Family
Reunion

Other books by Caroline B. Cooney

Family Reunion

Caroline B. Cooney

Delacorte Press

Published by
Delacorte Press
an imprint of
Random House Children's Books
a division of Random House, Inc.
New York

Visit us on the Web! www.randomhouse.com/kids
Educators and librarians, for a variety of teaching tools, visit us at
www.randomhouse.com/teachers

Cataloging-in-Publication Data is available from the Library of Congress.
ISBN 0-385-73136-1 (trade)
ISBN 0-385-90167-4 (GLB)

The text of this book is set in 11.5-point Joanna MT.

Book design by Kenny Holcomb

Printed in the United States of America

February 2004

10 9 8 7 6 5 4 3 2 1

BVG

Family
Reunion

Chapter One

It began when we found out that our new summer house had an old bomb shelter in the backyard, and my brother, Angus, decided to sell time-shares in it. Angus is twelve and a terrific salesman. He used to sell my Girl Scout cookies for me, and not once did a customer ask why a boy with a crew cut was in the Girl Scouts. He has red hair and freckles, and I think there is something about red hair and freckles that makes strangers relax their defenses and buy, buy, buy.

Soon after we examined our bomb shelter, Angus divided the year into fifty-two weeks and went off to sell ten shares per week of year-round, lifetime, come-as-you-are survival shelter use.

It was that "come-as-you-are" line that people liked. You could tell it soothed them to know that when the bomb fell, they wouldn't have to dress up to take advantage of their time-share.

"But Angus," I said. "What if the bomb falls in July and somebody bought a lifetime first-week-in-March use?"

Angus drew a long, slow, sad finger across his throat. "Poor planning," he told me. "People have to think ahead. Know their global politics." He turned to his latest potential buyer, an innocent Vermont child with an untouched allowance. "Or better yet," Angus said joyfully, "buy a share in each week of the year! That way you'll never have to worry."

Before Daddy found out and stopped him, Angus had sold seventy-two shares. He had even worked out the division of each shareholder's right to the cans of Campbell's soup still in the bomb shelter. I personally would be worried about chicken noodle soup from 1958.

Daddy went berserk. "We bought this summer house because you were going to enjoy fresh air! Swim in the lake! Fish for trout! Climb every mountain! People said that children need a backyard for a normal, stable upbringing, and so I said, Okay, June through August they'll have a backyard. I'll make these kids stable if it kills me. So what happens? You come up here from New York City, demoralize all these nice Vermont kids, rip off their allowances, and sell them . . ."

2

Daddy paused.

He was praying that Angus would admit he hadn't really sold time-shares to a bomb shelter; he had really gotten all that money from a paper route.

"Dad, it's a new idea," said Angus proudly. "A fresh concept. I bet nobody else in Vermont is doing it."

Daddy got a grip on himself and asked what Angus had been charging.

"Ten dollars a share, Dad. It's a bargain. Everybody saw that right off."

My father is a large man, well over six feet, with shoulders like a yardstick. Whenever he has to deal with Angus, he takes very deep breaths, so his chest rises, and his jacket lifts and his shirt buttons reach a state of high tension. I think of him as a rocket about to launch. I worry about the explosion.

"Angus," said my father, "we have hardly arrived in this town. So far I know the guy who installed the extra phone line, the mailman and the waitress at the coffee shop."

"Gee, Dad, that's a shame. I've met everybody. I've been going door-to-door for days."

Daddy's chest sank back to resting position. He looked up at the ceiling, which in our summer house is quite close to his head. He frequently communes with its cracks. Then he stared at his sweet-faced son and said he had just remembered pressing business back in New York City. He'd be gone for weeks. Possibly all summer. It was up to Angus and me and Annette (our stepmother) to go door-to-door, return all the money and apologize for anybody in our wholesome little family even thinking of selling bomb shares.

Angus had, however, earned seven hundred and twenty dollars. The thought of giving it back was not a happy one. He put on the expression of a puppy at the pound, entreating us to give him love and affection. Earnestly he explained that this sort of thing looked really great on a college application.

Daddy said this kind of thing would make any reasonable college admissions office bar the door.

Angus said he thought he would write Grandma about it, because Grandma was always proud of him, even if nobody else was.

Daddy said if Angus went and told Grandma, Daddy would kill him. Daddy's chest began expanding alarmingly. Angus backed up a bit.

I backed up completely and said I would go check the mail.

Mail is the best thing about having a summer house in Vermont. The big black box pokes up out of tall white daisies and high grass on the other side of a narrow country road, and when the little red flag is down, you know your mail has come.

Vermont is entirely treed. You'd think they had a genuine fear of open spaces and views. Trees curve in over roads and houses and towns, wave upon wave, as if local zoning laws require you to live in a green aquarium. Only the lake, being filled with water, is barren of trees.

I walked through the filtered sun and pulled down the little curved door of the black mailbox. I wasn't actually expecting any mail, because everybody we know uses e-mail or the phone. But there was a letter from Aunt Maggie.

Aunt Maggie is Daddy's older sister. She lives out in the Midwest, where she and her family lead A Perfect Life. We call them the Perfects, because it's rather like their real last name, which is Preffyn. In the old days, when we were sort of perfect ourselves, we used to visit them, but we don't anymore. Daddy says he doesn't have the energy.

Aunt Maggie married Uncle Todd, and she is lovely, and he is handsome, and she is chairman of the school board, and he is a pharmacist. They have a backyard, of course, have always had a backyard, and therefore their children, Brett and Carolyn, are also Perfect. Brett is sixteen and Carolyn is fourteen, and they never were awkward or fat, never had braces, never had pimples, never got anything below a B+. In gym they are always team captains. In photographs, they are always smiling and attractive. That is just the kind of family they are.

When they used to visit us in New York City, we would

walk down the sidewalk and point to perfectly innocent people waiting for the bus and whisper, "Careful. Drug deal." Carolyn and Brett always fell for that and told their mother, and Aunt Maggie would say that if we just had a backyard to play in, we would be stable, like her kids.

Stable is a big word in Aunt Maggie's life. She has stability, Carolyn and Brett have tremendous stability, but we have none. We are unstable, unbalanced and at risk.

Aunt Maggie loves that one. *At risk.* As if my brother and sister and I are poised at the edge of a cliff, teetering dangerously, nobody within reach to pull us away from a smushed-to-slush death.

When we were younger, you see, our mother fell in love with a dashing, romantic, handsome French newspaper reporter who at that time was covering the United Nations for a Paris paper. Mother left Daddy and went to live with Jean-Paul, and a few years later, they went on to Paris.

We stayed with Daddy. This was partly because we wanted to stay with Daddy and partly because Mother wasn't sure we would fit in with her new lifestyle. Although we could agree that Angus wouldn't fit easily into anybody's lifestyle, my sister, Joanna, and I did not like hearing that we wouldn't either.

Joanna, who is the oldest, is spending her entire summer with Mother and Jean-Paul. She is the first of us to visit France. Joanna left the very afternoon that school ended—

June 17—and won't be back until school starts again—September 8.

Daddy likes us to write to Mother, but I have a bad attitude toward this activity. A few weeks ago, I sat down at the computer and e-mailed Joanna (I don't correspond with my mother by any method) that Angus was enjoying his new leg.

Mother telephoned, which we don't do all that much because of the time difference and because Angus and I are apt to be rude. She demanded to know what had happened to Angus's old leg. Angus said it had gotten all crushed and thrown in the dump, but he had gotten a new one cheap, and Mother wasn't to worry about her share of the bill.

Mother telephoned Daddy at work for details. (It is hard to say which of them hates these phone calls more.) Of course, Daddy didn't know Angus had any fake legs, let alone cheap ones, so it was just the sort of conversation that had made Mother abandon Daddy in the first place. Mother called back to Vermont and demanded to speak to Annette about the leg, but Annette is afraid of Mother and whispered to Angus to say she wasn't home, and Angus of course said, "Annette says to tell you she's not home."

By then I don't think Mother really cared about Angus's leg. I think she called Daddy in New York again just to be difficult. This time Daddy remembered that Angus likes to use an old hollow detachable mannequin's leg as a briefcase or tote bag, down which he stuffs any papers he might need to carry around, such as the contracts for time-shares, although Daddy didn't know about those yet. Daddy gave Mother a sane, reasonable explanation for the leg story, but Mother did not think anybody in the picture was being either sane or reasonable.

But that was in the past.

Nobody cared about Angus's leg anymore. I just wanted to take the pressure off the bomb-share deals, so I ran into the house to read Aunt Maggie's letter out loud.

My father had sunk into the only chair in the summer house large enough to support him. Summer house furniture turned out to be flimsy, but Annette doesn't mind, as this means she gets to redecorate and replace all of it.

The house in Vermont has no curtains on any downstairs window. By day, the sun moves slowly from one pane of glass to the next. Hot little squares of sun first lie on the living room floor, then slide to the table, drift into the next room and become late-afternoon slants across the kitchen counters.

The heat of the day was already vanishing, and Daddy, exhausted from either his long drive or his children, was closing his eyes. The afghan on the back of the easy chair was pale blue with pink flowered trim. It sank down when Daddy did, and it lay around his shoulders like a baby blanket on a grizzly bear.

"You want to hear a letter from Aunt Maggie?" I said, but

I didn't give anybody a chance to say no. " 'Dear Brother Charlie,' " I read.

Daddy said that made him sound like an inmate at an institution. We did not tell him that he also looked like one, what with the baby blanket scootched around his cheeks.

" 'It is hard to believe, but Todd and I are approaching our twentieth wedding anniversary!!!!!!!!' " I read out loud. "Eight exclamation points," I told my listeners.

Enough to make anybody gag, but especially Daddy, who did not reach his first anniversary with Wife Number One, hit a twelfth with Wife Number Two (our mother) and is barely within reach of a second with Wife Number Three (Annette).

"Don't worry, Dad," Angus consoled him. "All those exclamation points mean that Aunt Maggie is as surprised as anybody that her marriage lasted all those years."

" 'And of course we want to have a big and wonderful family celebration of this unique event.' "

"Notice she's rubbing in how unique it is," said Daddy.

I kept reading. " 'So we've planned a family reunion gala for August!' "

My aunt Maggie is known for her enthusiasm, which tends to tire out everybody but Aunt Maggie. Now even her handwriting was bigger and more excited. I made a note to get a library book on handwriting analysis because I was sure there were depths to plumb in Aunt Maggie's.

" 'We're even getting in touch with all our old friends

from high school, Charlie!!!!!!!! We'll want everybody to come!! Joanna must fly back from Paris, and this will be our chance to get to know dear Annette at last, and how wonderful it will be for Shelley and Angus to be back in Barrington again!!!!' "

"Where they have all those backyards," said Angus.

Annette looked as if she would rather postpone meeting the Perfects for another generation or so. In her situation I would feel the same, since Annette does not measure up to anybody, especially Wife Number Two (Mother) and Aunt Maggie.

"What else is in the letter?" asked Angus. "It's awfully thick."

"The invitation the other several hundred people are getting," I said. "Miscellaneous driving directions and flying information, and the latest family photographs."

Annette began fussing with the Queen Anne's lace. Angus read that you can dye the flowers, so he has bunches of them sitting in glasses of water mixed with entire containers of food coloring. Nothing has happened with yellow or green, but red and blue have promise. The flower heads are now a sick pastel instead of white. Annette shifted Queen Anne's lace glasses all over the table.

"Can I telephone Joanna and tell her all about the family reunion?" I begged. "Please, please?"

Daddy looked wary. His usual excuse against phoning

Europe is the expense—therefore we should e-mail—but actually he's afraid Mother will be home and he'll have to talk to her, or worse, that Jean-Paul will answer and they'll have to have a civilized conversation. The crummy thing about divorce and remarriage is how you're required to be civilized about it and not scream ugly things, especially when several years have gone by and, if you have any stability at all, you have gotten over it.

"I'll tell Joanna you're not here," I said kindly.

Daddy was weak from dealing with Angus, and he agreed. I ran upstairs to use my own phone in the privacy of my bedroom. Vacation bedrooms are different from real bedrooms. In the New York apartment, my half of the room is lined with shelves and cabinets. Each shelf has a front and back layer of books, CDs, games I used to play, dolls I used to collect, papers I wrote last year. My drawers are stuffed with sweaters and sweatshirts, and socks pop out when I tug open the sock drawer. My view is limited to Joanna's side of the room, which is even more cluttered because she's had more years to clutter in. There is no visible wallpaper because we've been taping up posters for years without ever taking down the first ones, so formerly adored stars have only their feet showing beneath the hair of the currently adored star, who is partially obscured by the perfume advertisement Jo cut from a magazine and the cartoon I ripped from the Sunday comics.

In Vermont my room is bare. It has a gleaming wooden floor, white walls and nothing of me except my clothing, which is hidden in the closet and bureau. The view through two narrow windows, curtained with white, flower-sprigged muslin, is treetops. The leaves are not quiet. They shift as if they are straining to see more. In a high wind the leaves run in place, like basketball players hoping to get off the bench and into the game.

I sat cross-legged on the bed and dialed France.

I have this fear that Joanna will fit perfectly into Mother and Jean-Paul's lifestyle and will stay there forever and not come home in September. Every time I talk to her, she bubbles away about weekend visits to kings' castles, and dinners at ten P.M. and strolls in Paris, where she nibbles on a real croissant instead of the shabby make-believe ones we eat in New York. I am losing my sister. Joanna and I don't share a bedroom anymore, and she hasn't seen the bomb shelter or lived in the summer house, and she didn't help Angus divide up the Campbell's soup rights, and she probably thinks life is better abroad.

So actually, Aunt Maggie's Perfection was good timing. Joanna would have to come home nice and early, and we would all get very stable from all those Barrington backyards.

But when I read Aunt Maggie's letter to her, Joanna said, "August?" in a distracted voice. "Impossible, Shelley. Out of the question. Simply cannot. Jean-Paul and Mother and I will be spending the month traveling in the French mountains, with excursions into Switzerland and northern Italy. It's all arranged."

Outside, a chorus of insects rasped, as if planning an assault on the window screens. "You'd rather go to some dumb alp than have a watermelon-seed-spitting contest with Brett and Carolyn?" I said.

Joanna laughed. "Three years ago I thought it was crucial to win that contest. I was thirteen and immature. Now—well—admit it, Shell. You're just jealous of me."

I could not imagine being jealous of a person who had to spend week after week in the company of Mother and Jean-Paul and did not even get a break while he went off to work, but had to photograph an alp together.

"Daddy will make you come," I said, knowing he would not.

"He can't. It's Mother's time."

In divorce you cannot trespass on the other parent's time. It's a rule. Of course you do, all the time, but you do it quietly and sneakily. I sneakily let a quiver into my voice. "Jo, you have to come. Please. I need you. Angus needs you. We need to present a united front."

I am good at making people feel guilty. Once, my mother said she needed the Atlantic Ocean between us because of all the guilt I lay on her if she's any closer.

"Nonsense. You guys will be fine. Just leave Annette at home. She'll embarrass you if you bring her to Barrington."

I could not think of a way to leave my stepmother at home. "Lock her in a closet with enough water to last her a week?" I asked.

Joanna felt the plan deserved serious thought. She believes that Daddy's standards have fallen over the years. "Mother is incredibly more intelligent, beautiful, interesting and bilingual than Annette," she said.

"Annette is hardly even one-lingual," I admitted. "Especially after Angus works her over." I told Joanna about the bomb shares.

Joanna laughed. She has a wonderful laugh, loud and boisterous and room-filling. It hurt to listen to the laugh and know that it was really hundreds of miles away. Which would I rather have? I thought. A room to myself, with privacy and quiet and bare walls? Or Joanna doing her homework while she's online, borrowing my earrings while she's braiding my hair, sprawling all over my bed to eat her barbecue-flavored potato chips or Rice Krispies Treats or Oreo cookies? (She's never dumb enough to get crumbs on her own bed.)

"Oooooh!" whispered Joanna suddenly. "I just thought of something, Shelley. You know who else you might meet at a big reunion where they're inviting old high school friends? I bet you will finally meet Wife Number One."

Celeste.

We knew her name, but not her face; we knew the fact of her, but not the details. I have always been grateful to Celeste for preferring her career in Chicago over Daddy, because if she hadn't, we would not have been born. I think my father is perfect, and I cannot understand how Celeste, who knew him when he was so young and handsome, could have thought anything different. But it's good she did. I like myself and Joanna and even Angus with the exact gene assortment we have.

"I always used to think," said Joanna, her voice dreamily crossing two thousand miles of choppy blue ocean, "that Daddy and Celeste had a son they never told us about. A boy who must be a few years older than I am. Somehow I would meet him, all unaware, and we would fall in love, and I would end up marrying my half brother."

"Eeeeeuuuhhhh!" I shrieked. "How disgusting. How can you even think of things like that, Joanna? You know they didn't have any children."

"We know they didn't tell us if they had any," Joanna corrected me.

This was thrilling and repelling. A hidden, secret brother or sister.

"I have to go," said Joanna, and this time it was her voice with the quiver. "I love you, Shell."

"Wait! You haven't promised to come!"

"Loving you and coming to Barrington are separate issues. You think I want to hang around wringing the sweat out of my T-shirt on some deadly hot August afternoon while everybody tells Daddy how unstable we are? Forget it, Shell. You're on your own."

Chapter Two

Part of Daddy's stability program is fresh air, so Saturday morning, he took us on a hike at a state park, and we had our picnic at a famous revolutionary war battle site. Then we picked our own sweet corn at a farm where you can also pick your own zucchini, but even Daddy was against that.

Just when I thought we had had enough fresh air, we rented bicycles and pedaled uphill and down. Sunday we toured famous historical houses and noticed how small the beds were, and had the usual Early American House discussion on whether people were short back then or just slept all curled up.

Everybody was relieved when Daddy went back to New

York City before dawn Monday morning. His heart, he claimed, could not take the combination of Angus and all this rural green serenity. Our hearts were rather tired also, so we watched television all day Monday as an antidote to so much fresh air.

Annette didn't know what to do. This is frequently the case with Annette, which is kind of nice in a stepmother, because you can push her around so easily. How could she face people in this town? Her very first conversation would have to be about bomb shares.

"I wish you'd stop calling it a bomb share," said Angus. "I didn't sell a single person a share in a bomb. I sold them shares in a bomb *shelter*."

Annette said she thought I looked like the kind of person who would be good at returning shares to strangers who would probably get mad.

I have never been able to decide what I look like. I think I have potential. But I'm not there yet. When I look in the mirror, I see an unfinished product. Joanna says there is no such thing as a "finished" fourteen-year-old anyhow.

It's funny. I cannot do anything if I have to do it alone. But with a companion at my side, even a nutcase brother like Angus, I can take on the world. Or at least Vermont.

One way or another, you meet a lot of people through Angus. Everybody and their parents to whom shares had been sold wanted to stop and chat, see if Angus did this sort of thing routinely. Angus would lean on his leg, which he uses as a walking stick when he's in the mood, and fish ten dollars out of the hollow that runs from the mannequin's thigh to its toe, and solemnly hand it over.

You had your stock reactions: People fled or people started laughing.

There was one house where the grandfather, the father and the son were all named DeWitt, which appeared to be a first name. I narrowed my eyes at the DeWitt who was about my own age and wondered what it was like to be saddled with three generations of that ghastly name. Angus was returning ten dollars to DeWitt's little sister, Veronica. DeWitt said they'd take the ten dollars back only if they got a bomb-shelter tour. After I convinced Angus that no, he could not charge for the tour, DeWitt and Veronica fell in line behind us.

Eventually we collected quite a parade, everybody patiently waiting in front yards while Angus and I went up the steps to return ten dollars to the next victim. Some victims were edgy about opening the door under the circumstances, so Angus hollered loudly enough to do two houses at a time, and everybody in his parade clapped.

By the end of the week I felt as if we had lived in Vermont for years, and I am sure Vermont felt the same.

Annette steered clear of the village and all adults who might find out that she was responsible for the behavior of the kid with the leg and the bomb shelter. She did things like make grape jam, which we had known you could do, but had not known you could do *yourself*. We really got into it, stirring and sugaring and filling the cute little jelly jars, with their flat lids and separate screw tops.

But when it was time to have a peanut butter and jelly sandwich, Angus opted for brand names. He knew what was in those, he explained. He trusted them.

DeWitt and Veronica came in their rowboat and took us to their house around the far side of the lake so we could watch the movies they had rented. Each generation of DeWitt had a different taste in movies, so the selection was wide and interesting. Angus felt they should have an outboard motor on their boat, since oars were too tedious. DeWitt said *shhh*, because his grandfather DeWitt was at that very moment trying to Stop Noise Pollution On the Lake, perpetrated by people with outboard motors.

On Friday Daddy came up from the city with a huge bag of goodies from Zabar's, which is my favorite delicatessen in the world. I am sure that shopping at Zabar's on a regular basis makes you just as stable as all the backyards in Barrington. We had wonderful slabs of heavy country bread and four kinds of bagels and two flavors of cheesecake and several varieties of chocolate treats. When Daddy was very relaxed and having an Everything bagel slathered with Vermont butter and Annette's grape jam, not a combination beloved by many, Angus explained that some people didn't want their ten dollars back.

Daddy was suspicious. You get that way when you live with Angus.

"It's true," Annette said. "We had six who would rather keep their lifetime use of the bomb shelter."

We? I thought. I looked hard at Annette, but she did not own up to staying safely indoors during the entire bomb-shelter-return time span.

"Probably going to rent their shares out to some passing skier in February," muttered my father. "I can see the newspaper ad now: Unique accommodations. Cozy underground space. Free soup."

Angus thought this was possibly the most brilliant idea our father had ever had. "And here I thought you were some dull businessman in New York," said Angus wonderingly, offering to shake Daddy's hand. "We'd better put the ad in the paper now, Dad. People will be wanting to make their winter plans."

My father stared out the window into the dark. In Vermont, after the sun vanishes, the grass goes black and the trees and the lake turn indigo, like blue-stained shadows, but the sky is translucent. You can see through its holes to the stars, as if the night is an old skirt with a silver slip. "Maybe when we visit Barrington, somebody there will offer to keep Angus," Daddy said.

Annette said that from what we had told her of Barrington, they did not grow people like Angus there.

"New blood," said my father hopefully. "They need an infusion of—"

"I'm old blood, Dad," said Angus. "I'm practically a native of that town."

"You've been there maybe five times," said our father. "Six, tops." He threatened Angus with bodily mutilation if Angus brought up the ski rental idea again. He said Angus would resemble that leg he carried around, severed at important junctions of his body. Annette said nervously that this was just the sort of talk we must be sure to avoid around the Perfects.

I have always wanted to be part of a big family. I used to think that if we had just moved to Barrington, or if we were Wife Number One's children and Daddy never reached Two and Three, then we would never have left Barrington, and my cousin Carolyn and I would hang out together.

I wondered what Brett and Carolyn did all day long in Barrington. It's a pretty town. Huge oaks and maples divide the wide, flat front yards, and there are bushes as big as bunk beds for when you're playing hide-and-seek. Although we were all too old for those games now. Barrington River is too swift for swimming, but there are town pools and a terrific mall, a pretty little downtown and a brick elementary school, like the ones in picture books.

Carolyn and Brett have rope swings and a hammock, a tire swing and an ancient sandbox, mainly used by cats. I remember those things from our last visit, when I was eleven and Mommy and Daddy had separated, and everybody was saying how terrible it was, and it *was* terrible. I sat in Grandma's lap and cried, and she had a big white wicker rocking chair and we rocked and rocked.

My grandparents used to live in a house just like DeWitt's, with brown shingles and big porches. The porch ceiling was painted light blue, like morning sky, and the floor was painted gray, and everything was peeling. Once on a rainy day we roller-skated for hours, wearing dents in the porch floor. Grandma just smiled and made more lemonade.

I always think of Barrington like that. It's always summer, and we're always drinking lemonade, and Grandma is always giving me a hug.

But Grandpa died, and Grandma moved to Arizona to escape the harsh winters. Somebody bought their house and put yellow siding over the shingles and took off one porch and added skylights. I saw it in a photograph, but I don't want to see it in real life, because I'm afraid of losing the memory of the brown house where Grandpa lived and Grandma hugged and Mommy and Daddy were still married.

We sat quietly while Daddy had his iced tea and Angus

and I had ripe red cherries from the bowl Annette had put on the table among the pastel Queen Anne's lace. Angus and I collected the cherry pits in a cup he had made by sawing off the bottom of a plastic soda bottle. He was going to plant the pits in the gutter to see if they would root in the rotting leaves Daddy had not yet cleaned out. This was a project that would involve the danger of falling and would have to be done when Daddy was in New York and Annette was shopping.

I imagined the August reunion.

The Perfects would be all lined up, clean and calm and camera-ready. Their clothes would match and might even be ironed. Everybody would have had a haircut the day before.

We would be a shambles. Angus would wave his leg, and Annette would be dull. Daddy would look like an illustration from "The Three Bears," and I would be herding my family into place, like a little sheepdog.

"Did you sign up for the library summer reading program?" asked our father. He probably figured any children's activity at a Vermont library had to be safe.

"Yes!" cried Angus, with whom nothing is safe. "They're doing unusual pets. Mine will win all the prizes."

It is always Angus's intention to win all the prizes. He gets one now and then, usually from a science teacher who is just praying he will go away.

The library here has only two rooms: children's and

grown-ups', divided by the circulation desk. The children's room is old and soft, with dark wood walls and old wood tables. I love it there. But I was not in the summer reading program. The librarian said I was too old. He waved me away from the safe little shelf of choices for summer readers and shooed me into adult books. I don't like real adult books. My reading tastes had frozen at the third-grade level, and I read exclusively those books where everybody lives happily ever after and not much goes wrong in the middle either.

"What pets?" said Annette, puzzled.

"Wait here," Angus ordered her, and he raced down to the basement and came up a few minutes later with a box he had constructed by soldering together cookie sheets and an old metal-framed window. It was rickety, with a sideways list. He had attempted to correct this with duct tape and a piece of kindling. "Look," he whispered.

Through the glass wall of his box, you could see two little dark things racing around.

"Cockroaches!" screamed Annette.

Angus beamed at her. "Good for you," he complimented her. "They're very smart, you know. When the world ends, they won't. They've been here since dinosaurs. The librarian said that was very clever of me, bringing my own cockroaches from home." Angus stared admiringly into his shaky box.

Annette yelled that we didn't have any cockroaches in

either of our homes. She wanted to know how she could even enter the library now to borrow a simple mystery novel when the librarian thought our house was full of cockroaches and the other patrons thought we routinely sold shares in bombs.

Angus waved away her distress. He said the librarian was a great guy who really believed Angus would be able to train his cockroaches to run along the sidewalks Angus had constructed from shoe-box rims inside the cookie-sheet container.

Daddy said he felt tired, and if the cockroaches were secured for the night, he would just go lie down. Annette said she didn't care how secure the cockroaches were: Either the roaches were leaving the house this instant or she was.

Of course any stepchild worth his red blood likes this kind of threat from a stepmother.

Angus and I really got into the idea of Annette leaving and the roaches staying, which led Daddy to take Annette out for a late dinner while Angus and I stayed home to make ourselves grilled cheese. This was not enough supper, so we had cold cereal with bananas, and that wasn't enough, so we defrosted a Pepperidge Farm cake and split that. Then we had had enough.

Monday Daddy went back to New York again.

Angus agreed to keep the roaches at the library, and the librarian told Annette that in spite of everything, she could go on borrowing books because it is a free country.

Annette said she would prefer to be welcomed for some reason other than constitutional requirements, but at least she would have enough to read now.

Joanna's next e-mail read:

Dear Shell—I have rules for you. Promise you'll keep them at this reunion. First, stick up for Mother. Don't let them say anything bad about her. Real mothers don't give up custody, and Aunt Maggie is bound to harp on that. Harp right back. Don't let them say anything bad about Daddy either. That will be tricky because they'll certainly want to say something bad about somebody. Get them started on Annette. That should keep everybody busy for the week you're there. I'm so glad I'll be on another continent. I'll be spared all that talk about what hard lives we've led and how remarkable that we've come through so well. Barrington will be a zoo. Enjoy. What kind of presents do you want me to buy you while I'm shopping in interesting places and you're in Barrington? Love, Joanna

DeWitt and Veronica began showing up rather frequently. All I had to do was sit on the edge of our dock with my toes in the water, and DeWitt and his little sister would appear in one of their boats. It was rather magical, as if mixing nail polish with Vermont lake water brought boys into your life.

"Hi," said DeWitt. "Your brother up to anything?"

"Why? Is your summer going slowly?"

"It's always slow here," said DeWitt. "This is our forty-eighth summer at the lake."

"You don't look middle-aged."

"My grandparents own the house. They bought it when they were young. All summer long is one big family reunion. The kids stay while the parents rotate in and out on weekends or during their vacations." DeWitt waved across the lake to his huge brown-shingled place, with all its screened porches to combat Vermont flies and gnats and mosquitoes. A safe house, where families had reunions but never split up.

"It's an off month, though," said DeWitt gloomily. "Not one of my seventeen cousins is here. It's just me and the creep." He pointed to Veronica, who seemed proud to have any label at all, including creep.

An off month. What if we had an off reunion? What if they didn't make their own lemonade anymore, pressing lemon halves down on the old glass squeezer in the pantry, but just bought their lemonade in a carton?

"So it's just me and my sister," said DeWitt. "I'm bored."

I nodded. In real life, as opposed to summer-on-the-lake life, a fifteen-year-old boy does not play with his seven-year-old sister or notice his fourteen-year-old neighbor. But we were acceptable as summer filler.

DeWitt was from New York too, so we exchanged neighborhood and school information, and DeWitt said he wouldn't be coming next summer because he'd have a terrific job instead. I have never wanted a job. I don't mind it when other people work, but I don't want to participate.

I think life should be set up so you can choose where to pause. I am the only person I know who loved middle school, and I would have been willing to stay there indefinitely, being an eighth grader. Eighth is such a relaxing year. You study only what you've studied before. I like that. When I said so to DeWitt, he narrowed his eyes, and shortly after receiving this information, he paddled away with his sister. DeWitt was the kind of person who would always be panting for the next stage, like Joanna, while Angus is the kind of person who is so busy in the moment, he forgets past and future. And I am the kind of person who wants to sit and think, watch and wonder, without really participating all that much.

Down on the dock where I lay watching DeWitt row, there was not the slightest breeze, but in the blue sky a strong wind rushed clouds along, as if they had an urgent commitment in another world.

I moseyed back into the house, where Angus was licking

icing from a cake Annette had baked. There's something about a summer house that entices you into the kitchen. The night before, we had been up for hours making corn tassel dolls because I had read about them in an ancient Lois Lenski book. Maybe Vermont hours are slower than New York hours, or perhaps Vermont kitchens are roomier and sunnier.

Angus ran a finger around the cake rim and scooped up a dollop for me. I licked it off his finger. Yummy. "You know what Joanna said to me the other day, Angus?" I said. I took my own icing scoop. There were now sled tracks where our fingers had plowed and the chocolate-cake earth showed through.

"What?" Angus got milk out of the refrigerator.

"She said she's always wondered if Daddy has a son by his first marriage, and she would meet the son and have a crush on her own brother." I poured us each a glass of milk. "Isn't that silly, Angus? The whole idea of Daddy having another son?"

Angus gave me a funny look. "But Shelley," he said, "Dad does have another son. His name is Toby."

Chapter Three

Vermont was quiet, the sun hot, the lake shining. Down by the water Annette turned a page in her book.

"What are you talking about?" I whispered.

"Toby," my brother repeated unhelpfully.

"Toby who?" I demanded.

"I don't know. I just know he is."

"Is what?" I was shrieking now, but still whispering. Annette was aware of nothing. For that matter, Angus was aware of nothing. He began gathering supplies for one of his endless projects. I followed him. He rounded up two pairs of sunglasses, one to wear and one to perch in his hair. The pair he was wearing had miniature green venetian blinds, so I had to look through slots to see his eyes. "*Dad does have another son,*" I quoted. "*His name is Toby*. What kind of sentences are those?"

Angus pawed through the rainy-day box of broken crayons, dry Magic Markers, tracing paper and construction paper. It had been abandoned by the previous summer-home owner, and we hadn't discarded it, because you never knew when you might need a coloring book. Angus extracted some relatively clean paper and fished around for pencils.

"Angus! Exactly how did you learn about Toby? Give me all the details. Now."

Angus shrugged. "Don't know the details." He checked the pencils to see how sharp their tips were.

"You do too know. If you don't give me a real answer, I'll stab you with your pencils. Information as important as that would stick with you. Especially with you. I bet you have a whole separate file in your computer for family secrets."

Angus looked thoughtful. He's always ready for a new project. But he shrugged a second time. "I have to get downtown," he informed me, although *downtown* is a rather strong word for this village. "I can't waste more time on this." From the stack of folded aluminum outdoor chairs, he chose a low folding beach chair, the kind where your bottom practically touches the sand. He gathered his necessities, slinging the flimsy beach chair over his shoulder like a huge purple-and-green-striped handbag. I wondered why he was not using his leg, but if I mentioned it, he'd remember the leg, and I could always hope that he was on the downside of leg-carrying.

I gripped his arm, but Angus threw me off. Last year he was a scrawny, thin, weak eleven-year-old. This year he's still thin, but he can pin me to the wall or the floor or, I suppose, the lake bottom should he choose. I'm against it. Little brothers should stay little.

"Nobody can have a son and not mention him!" I cried. "How about Christmas presents? Birthdays? And there's money! You have to pay for new shoes and braces and band instruments. And wouldn't Grandma and Grandpa have noticed and said something? And Mother—during the divorce, our divorce—wouldn't Mother have mentioned that? She mentioned everything else on earth. She would have thrown in a son named Toby. I think you're making it up, Angus, and I think it's mean and cruel and horrible, and I want the truth."

Angus hates to repeat himself. He always wants a conversation to be brand-new. "So ask Dad. He'll be home Friday night. I'll get Annette out of the way."

Angus was truly not interested. He was interested in the money in little Vermont pockets, and he was interested in cockroaches, but he was not interested in his own incredible remark. "But Shelley, Dad does have another son. His name is Toby."

Angus ran upstairs, and I could tell he was rooting around in Daddy and Annette's room. He came down with a pair of binoculars.

He was now burdened with the sort of collection that makes an older sister nervous, because who could guess what this latest project might be and where he was planning to put that beach chair? Experience told me not to go along. I tried to see into his eyes, but the sunglasses kept his secrets. I resent sunglasses when other people wear them. They could be laughing at you or ignoring you and you can't ever know. Black lids or silver reflections replace their eyes, as if they are part robot. When people wearing sunglasses speak to you, you want to wrench the things off their faces.

But if you wear them, you live in another world, safe in your own dark.

You should always be able to wear your sunglasses, but other people should never be allowed to wear theirs.

In the kitchen, Angus looked around for a nice portable snack. I tried to think of a threat that would force him to talk, but Annette walked in. Angus stood in front of the cake so she wouldn't spot our ski trails in the snow icing. "I'm going to walk down to the village and go to the library," she told us. We just nodded. She hesitated, hoping one of us would want to go with her, I suppose, or at least say something nice, but I was frozen by the specter of Toby, and Angus was too busy with his own plans.

Annette left the house, pausing at the clump of orange tiger lilies at the edge of the yard. She loved them and had tried putting them in bouquets, but they didn't last.

I thought she would never be out of sight and hearing range. I turned to interrogate Angus, but he was gone, having taken the other door, and was marching off by himself. He never cares what he looks like and never cares whether anybody goes with him. I like to have a friend along. In fact, if I don't have a friend along, I probably won't go.

I cut myself a piece of cake. I drank my milk. I walked outside.

The hedge was woven with honeysuckle and bees. Perfume and humming crossed in the soft air. Waves made by a passing motorboat lapped over smooth stones. I lay on my back in the high grass and planned my conversation with Daddy. So, Dad. How was work? Spoken to Toby lately?

I wasn't lonely out there in the grass. How can you be lonely when the sun is beating down on you? But I was alone and afraid of what Angus had said. Fear isn't like sunglasses. Fear brings darkness, but a dark full of menace instead of safety.

I tried to think of safe things. If only my friends from New York were here—Marley or Kelsey or Bev. We would talk about clothes. What to pack for this family reunion halfway across the nation with four people named Perfect.

Summer linen jackets or stained T-shirts? Graceful sun-dresses or torn jeans?

The day crept on, slow and hot.

I thought of Barrington, of barbecues and cornfields. Brett was sixteen and would have interesting friends who might think I was cute. Grandma always had great presents. Aunt Maggie fixed breathtaking amounts of food, as if she thought you couldn't eat well in New York.

The sun faded and the sky became pale and flat, a sheet hung out to dry. My world felt emptied, as if Angus had punctured it. Toby—whoever and whatever and if ever he was—was under all my thoughts, like water under a boat. From your boat you can stare at the sky or lean into your oars, but the water is always there, deep and cold and dark. Because I had no one with whom to share my thoughts, they were less—but at the same time, more, because they weren't diluted by being hashed over.

I went inside and telephoned Joanna. I didn't care about the time difference, and neither did she. When the phone rings, answer it; who cares what time it is?

She had just been to Monet's garden and strolled among the very flowers he had planted and painted, and she was eager to tell me all about it.

"I don't care about anything French," I told her. "Angus says there really is a brother we don't know about, and his name is Toby."

"Oh, please. Angus is just one tall tale after another. Less loving sisters than we are would call him an out-and-out liar."

"But you guessed the same thing, Joanna. It must have been based on something. What did you hear once?"

"I don't know," she said uneasily. "I'm sure I made it up, Shell."

"Go ask Mother what she knows."

But Joanna didn't want to start anything.

"If Toby doesn't exist, you won't be starting anything."

"If he does exist and Mother never heard of him and she gets mad at Dad for never telling her, it'll be awful, Shelley. But stop worrying about it. It's a typical Angus rumor." She changed the subject. She wanted to talk about boys. Joanna always has lots of admirers. She and Daddy argued solidly the year she was fifteen because he wouldn't let her go out except in a group until she was sixteen. To celebrate turning sixteen, she telephoned every boy she'd been forced to refuse and assigned one night to each boy.

Joanna and Angus are never shy. I can't imagine asking a boy out. I can't imagine asking my father if he has another boy of his own. One he somehow forgot to mention.

"So," said Joanna. "Any boys on the scene?" She had already dismissed the Toby story. But then, she is never taken in by Angus, and I always am. "There's a kid named DeWitt," I told her. "He paddles around now and then."

Sure that I was in the throes of first love, Joanna demanded a physical description. I had not really bothered to look at DeWitt. "He's—well—he's this—you know—I don't know; I think he has a tan."

"Oh, well," said Joanna. "I suppose you're going to be a late bloomer."

I would be the quiet bud amidst the splendor of flowers. Just as early-bloomer blossoms fade, petals wilting, stems dropping, I would come out—beautiful and strong in the setting sun: the Late Bloomer. All the boy flowers would look up, startled, and move toward me in the evening.

Joanna admitted that even she was not blooming well in Paris, where there were tons of boys, but they didn't gather around, and she had no friends her age. I felt better about Paris. Joanna wouldn't stay very long where the boys didn't gather around. I told her how my thoughts had been less when I had nobody to share them with, and yet more, because they weren't diluted.

"Like concentrated juice," agreed Joanna, "all your thoughts jammed into one frozen cylinder. But if you have friends to talk it over with, then it's the whole gallon. You could pour off glasses and glasses without even noticing. So your thoughts are more important when you keep them to yourself."

"Oh, Joanna, you have to come to the reunion! I don't want to be all concentrated and lonely. I want to pour off my thoughts on you."

"No."

So we ended our phone call with a nice screaming fight just like old times, and I went back out into the yard feeling good again.

Annette and Angus came home together. They were both crying. I had never seen Annette break down, and Angus probably hasn't cried since preschool. The dust from the road had swirled up around their faces and caked in the tear tracks. They looked like relatives by blood instead of by marriage.

"How dare you spy on me?" said Annette, sobbing. "You are horrible, Angus!"

"I wasn't spying on you!" he said, weeping. "I really wasn't. I was taking notes and making lists. I had a list of feet. I'm thinking of manufacturing a new type of sneaker, and I had to get a good count of what people are wearing. Then, since we're eating so much up here, I figured I might as well keep track of weight while I was at it. What proportion of people in Vermont eat too much? Of course I always carry my license plate list with me, like there's a dentist and his plate reads GUM DZZZ and you never know when you might find another really good plate like that, so—"

"You were not!" screamed Annette. "You were spying on me. I came out of the psychiatrist's office and you had your binoculars trained on me."

"It was a coincidence," whispered Angus. "It really was. I didn't know where you were. Don't tell Dad, Annette."

Luckily I hadn't devoured all of Annette's cake. Quickly I passed out slices, adding scoops of chocolate ice cream and glasses of milk all around, and told Annette that Angus and I loved her cake, that we had sneaked half the cake already because it was so unbelievably scrumptious. Then I ruined it. "Why are you going to this shrink?" I asked.

"You think it's going to be easy for me to face all those people in Barrington? You don't call them Perfect for a joke. They are Perfect. And they all think that your father's first . . . well—"

"Two wives," I supplied.

"Were so terrific," she finished. "And I'll have to show up with you two, and Angus will probably take his leg and—"

"They won't hold *you* responsible for my leg!" cried Angus. "They'll say it's just another sign of our unstable life."

"They'll say *I'm* another sign of your unstable life," said Annette, reaching for a tissue.

We all dipped into the Kleenex box and mopped up. We finished the cake crumbs. Annette said were there any onion bagels left? and Angus said no, and I said, "Anyway we're out of cream cheese." Annette checked the discarded Zabar's bag in the garbage that had held the onion bagels, and I said Boston was only two hours away, as opposed to New York, which was five, and they probably had a decent deli in Boston, and Annette said, "Let's go."

So we all got in the car and drove to Boston to find a delicatessen.

"You know," said Angus, "you're not bad, Annette."

"I know my delis," she agreed. "There are those like you, Angus, who can scent a profit." (Angus's chest expanded, like Dad's.) "And those like you, Shelley, for whom adorable teenage boys row across lakes." (I tried again to remember anything about DeWitt except his tan.) "But I myself am a delicatessen-finder of the very highest order." Taking a pen from her handbag, Annette drew a first-prize blue ribbon on her napkin and draped it over her shoulder.

"Then I think Dad was wise to marry you," said Angus. "Because that is a valuable skill."

Chapter Four

Angus opened a roadside stand to sell scarlet and orange zinnias he cut in the back garden. For hours he sat surrounded by iced tea bottles, soup cans and pickle jars filled with water and flowers, holding a pink-striped beach umbrella over himself to keep off the sun. When cars did not stop at the rate he wanted, Angus changed tactics. He threw his umbrella down and rushed out into the road, arms waving frantically.

Of course they braked now. This adorable redheaded son of America probably needed either an ambulance or adoption. (Annette voted for adoption.)

The people in one car (New York plates) thought Angus's

zinnias were a free Welcome to Vermont gift and drove off without paying, telling each other how sweet it was up here in the country.

The people in the next car (New York plates) thought two dollars was an awful lot to ask for half-wilted zinnias and drove off without paying, telling each other what a shame it was that even here in Vermont children would try to rip you off.

Annette spent the day pretending she didn't know what Angus was doing. She had a scrap of yellow-and-blue fabric, which she held up to the kitchen windows and walls to see if she could live with it.

I spent the day being jealous of Angus for having the kind of personality that could get away with anything, and make up anything, and fear nothing.

"Angus!" yelled Annette. "It's getting late. Come on in to help with supper."

Angus's idea of helping with supper was to put so much lighter fluid on the briquettes that the flames reached the roof. I was not surprised that Annette had stopped serving hamburgers and moved on to safer food items. "We'll have spaghetti and pesto sauce with fresh basil," she said.

In New York you can get fresh basil any day of the year, twenty-four hours a day, but somehow in New York our hours would be more precious, and we'd just buy it made.

If we lived in Barrington, I thought, we'd have dinner at

Aunt Maggie's a lot, and Uncle Todd would cook on one of those huge outdoor grills, and we'd be assigned to bring the salad, because Aunt Maggie would figure that even an unstable family such as ours could throw lettuce into a bowl. After supper all the cousins would play a long, slow board game like Monopoly, which we cannot play even in Vermont because we get so determined to win that we turn into rabid beasts and Annette quits.

Angus stomped into the kitchen. "How can I get rich selling zinnias?" he shouted. "Dad ruined all the real chances of earning real money. I hate Vermont." He slammed the door and kicked the table leg. "I don't want spaghetti, either! I want a tuna fish, peanut butter and Fluff sandwich."

"That's disgusting," said Annette.

"You're disgusting," said Angus.

I wondered if the Perfects had conversations like this. I got the spaghetti box out of the pantry. Italian food is so comforting. That little slurp of spaghetti trailing into your mouth, the little flecks of sauce zinging across the table if you are Angus, who is a high-speed slurper—these can always be counted upon.

Angus yelled at Annette for marrying Daddy. Annette yelled at Angus for never cooperating, never trying, never even being human like normal twelve-year-old boys.

I put large handfuls of stiff spaghetti into the boiling water, poking it down with a wooden spoon. I questioned whether twelve-year-old boys were ever human or normal.

Angus yanked the peanut butter off the shelf and began slathering it an inch thick on bread as he told Annette what he thought of her.

"How about a knuckle sandwich?" I said to my brother, forgetting how strong he had gotten. I slugged him and he slugged me back, and then I was afraid for my life. I screamed for Annette to protect me, but of course she didn't feel this was her responsibility. I put the table between myself and Angus, who tried to flip the table and crush me with it. Glasses of Queen Anne's lace hit the floor.

"Stop it!" yelled Annette.

We didn't stop.

"At least don't fall into the boiling water," she said.

The phone rang.

I thought it was Daddy phoning from Canada, where he had gone on business. Each of us wanted to get our version of the fight in first, and we all dove for the phone. Annette slipped on a patch of Kool-Aid powder from when Angus had been trying to have a combination Kool-Aid and zinnia stand. Angus slipped in the lace water. I got the phone. But it was not Daddy.

"Granger Elliott here," said a man's deep voice. "Annette Fletcher, please."

Fletcher was Annette's maiden name, and Granger Elliott was her boss before she quit to marry Daddy. He'd been at the wedding. He knew her name was Wollcott now. I glared at the phone, and just to be difficult, I put him on speaker phone instead of handing the receiver to Annette, who was on the floor recovering.

Nobody was as competent as Annette, Granger Elliott told her, and therefore us, because he thought his conversation was private. Nobody understood the job. Nobody could replace her. Wouldn't she please, please, please come back to him? She could name her price. He needed her.

Angus helped Annette to her feet. Angus righted the table. I picked up the glasses. Angus got a mop. I stirred the spaghetti. Angus *used* the mop.

At the office, I thought, nobody will demand tuna fish, peanut butter and Fluff sandwiches. Nobody will sell bomb shares. Nobody will row Annette into the middle of the lake just as a thunderstorm is boiling up, and then dive out and swim home, abandoning her, a woman who can't row, hates the water and feels the lake is out to get her. And then she's right.

My hand was bruised from belting Angus. Brett and Carolyn probably never beat on each other. Never even threw their dirty socks at each other. Probably never got the socks dirty to start with.

Angus opened a jar of Ragú tomato sauce, having a low opinion of pesto. It popped when he broke the seal, and he licked the inside of the cap. Angus likes his tomato sauce cold.

Of course Annette would go back to work. We'd have one mother overseas and a stepmother at the office. I'd be home with Angus after school, fighting over television rights and snacks. Next summer we wouldn't be able to come to Vermont. We'd sell the summer place, because there wouldn't be a grown-up to stay there with us. For a week or two we'd get shipped to Barrington, where everybody would know we were visiting because our actual family didn't have time for us.

I ripped open a bag of potato chips so savagely that it burst and spewed chips all over the damp kitchen. Annette turned her back on the sight and clicked off the speaker phone. Of course we could still hear her end fine. "I'm willing to discuss it," she told Granger Elliott in the voice of one who is willing to accept a handful of diamonds. "I can drive down to the city tonight, and first thing in the morning we can meet at the office and hammer out the details. We have to be done by noon so that I can drive back here for dinner tomorrow."

She's not too eager, is she? I thought.

Annette hung up, and when she looked around the kitchen, I didn't think she was looking at us or the mess or the various dinner choices. She was looking for her car keys. "I'll call the Frankels next door," she said. "They won't mind if you spend the night. Go get your sleeping bags."

Angus hears only what he wants to hear. "Oh, good," he said. "We're going to New York. I've always wanted to eat spaghetti in the car. I'll drink it from a glass."

"You're staying here," said Annette.

"You can't leave us here!" said Angus.

Annette was already on the phone with the neighbors, who were obviously going along with the plan. "Thanks a million. They'll be there in a minute," said Annette.

"I'm going with *you*!" yelled Angus.

"No. I have things to think about. I don't need the two of you bickering in the backseat, demanding to stop at every McDonald's and changing the radio station every ten miles." She found her purse, checked to be sure she had her ATM cards and credit cards and jingled her car keys. She was traveling light. "Finish your dinner," she said, although nobody had started yet. "Then get your sleeping bags and go over to the Frankels'."

Angus threw his zinnia money down. It spattered over the room, one quarter spinning madly in the center of the floor. "I hate you! You're always pushing us around. You won't even let us go to New York and it's our house there, not yours. When I grow up, I'll never come near you. Never!"

Annette shrugged.

Angus turned and ran out of the house. The screened door slammed so hard it bounced two times. Angus's feet pounded for a moment over the porch and steps, and then the sound was swallowed up in the deep grass. Annette put her hands over her eyes and took a deep breath. Then she looked around at the chaos of the kitchen. Evidence of the food fight was everywhere.

"I'll clean it up," I told her.

"Where do you think Angus went?" she asked.

"Outside behind a bush, waiting for you to leave so he can drink his spaghetti and fix his tuna peanut butter Fluff sandwich for dessert."

I know it did not cross Annette's mind that we might want her to stay home with us. We told her daily that we would never miss her.

She drove off into the night.

The house seemed darker. I cleaned slowly. I love how things get clean, how they sparkle and shine. If only I could get my thoughts like that, bleached free of the sadness that was chewing on me right now. Outside, the lake lapped and the wind blew. An insect chorus screamed hoarsely.

There was nothing between me and the night except flimsy screens on open windows. I was desperate for company. "Angus!" I called. "Angus!"

He didn't answer. I tried again later, and he still didn't answer. I offered food, and he didn't answer. Angus was good and mad not to come back for food. I was afraid to close the windows and afraid to turn my back on the door, which I couldn't lock, because Angus had to get back in. I wrapped myself in the plaid football blanket for protection and turned on the TV for company. Lying on the sofa with my spine pressed into the pillows, I tried not to think about the black gaping holes of the house, where darkness sat looking in at me.

"Shelley! Shelley!" Mrs. Frankel was shaking my shoulder. "Shelley, you and Angus were supposed to come over to our house ages ago. It's late. There isn't a light on in your entire house. How long have you been asleep? And where is Angus?"

Chapter Five

We did not find Angus.

"Let's not get frantic," said Mrs. Frankel, who was frantic. "He's got to be here. Let's stay very, very, very calm." She skittered around our house, bumping into lights like a moth. She had been wearing a huge T-shirt in place of pajamas, over which she now had her beach robe. Finally she pulled on jeans and a pair of lime green linen summer sandals. She looked peculiar but comforting, the way people do when they have forgotten appearances and conventions. I hung on to my plaid stadium blanket and the Frankels.

Mr. Frankel drove the quarter mile to the village as if

Angus might be sitting on the curb. Our voices pierced the night—"Angus! Angus!"—but the night remained soft and warm and unworried, a façade of dark leaf and silent lake, behind which the blackness of evil crouched.

When he got home without finding Angus, Mr. Frankel put new batteries into his flashlight and walked along the shore, casting the beam over the water, as if expecting to see Angus's sneakers sticking up. He went down the docks, poking his light into rowboats. Neighbors emerged to help. "Angus?" they said, nodding, as if they had been expecting this sooner or later. "Has he run away?"

Running away was not Angus's style.

"Hitchhiking?" they asked.

I could imagine Angus hitchhiking. I could imagine him not caring in the least where he ended up. Or with whom. I could imagine him shrugging about any precaution, skipping anything sensible, laughing off any warning sign.

The police arrived quickly. A little boy vanished after midnight had not only brought the two on duty but also roused dozens of volunteer firemen and rescue workers from their beds, as if they expected the worst. But once I described us, it was clear that my family was the thing that was worst. *Twelve-year-old boy, red hair, ninety pounds, ran away from home. Father out of the country, mother lives abroad, stepmother driving in the middle of the night to New York City, abandoned care of children to* neighbors they scarcely know, fourteen-year-old sister left in charge fell asleep.

"Broken family," said the police, nodding. "New Yorkers."

I flushed in the darkness of our yard. I felt responsible for the moral character of all New York City.

Mr. Frankel searched for Daddy's Montreal hotel phone number. I had Annette's cell phone number by memory, but I couldn't bear to give it out. She would be halfway there, having escaped our clutches, driving toward the salvation of her old life, and now she would be accused of abandoning her stepchildren.

The untouched spaghetti was congealed and pasty white. The jar of sauce lay on its side, telling all the world we were the sort of people who ate out of cans and whose parents didn't leave phone numbers. The volunteers were sent to search terrifying places. The trunks of neighbors' cars. The town dump. The trash alley behind the village stores.

DeWitt and his father and grandfather DeWitts showed up. They looked not at all alike, the grandfather tall and silvery and trim, the father short and stocky and dark, and my DeWitt just plain wonderful. Annette had been right. He was adorable. "You okay, Shelley?" he asked.

Nobody had worried about me. Angus's situation had taken up all the worry energy. "Kind of," I said.

He touched my shoulder, just fingertips, just the slightest

suggestion of pressure, but I almost wept to have him there, a true ally. I did not permit myself to cry, though. It would have been unstable.

DeWitt said, "I know this is dumb, Shell; I know it was the very first place you looked. But . . . you did check the bomb shelter, didn't you?"

The following day was gray and misty. Daddy sat out on the dock talking on the phone with Annette, who seemed reluctant ever to drive back to Vermont and join us.

I had an early breakfast, and then I also had a late breakfast while Angus taped a PBS rerun that featured a rain dance. Then he watched it seventy-five times in a row until he had it memorized.

I e-mailed Joanna, sparing her no detail of the night before.

We found Angus wrapped in a green army blanket I didn't know we owned, but it came with the bomb shelter. He was asleep on that army-issue cot. He was disgusted with us for being upset, and he wouldn't apologize to anybody for giving us all heart attacks. He said we should have known he was in his bomb shelter. Even one of the firemen said we should have known. The fireman's daughter

turned out to be one of the ones who refused
to take back her ten dollars. The fireman
said now that he was getting a good look at
the salesman of the time shares, he thought
maybe it wasn't the survival aspect that had
his daughter's attention. Of course Angus
gagged and moaned at the idea that girls
might enter his life in the shape of—well—
girls. All the neighbors and rescuers were
too wired to go home and sleep, so we par-
tied instead. One good thing about Annette:
She fell in love with the whole pantry
concept. You would not believe how much
snack food was sitting in that pantry,
waiting for us to feed twenty people. Mrs.
Frankel wouldn't serve anybody who had said
anything bad about New York City, so all the
Vermonters who were rude had to apologize.
It turned out half of them were former New
Yorkers anyway and had been feeling pretty
guilty.

Joanna answered right away.

I am so glad I am not there. Angus is just
a form of portable public humiliation. But

> there is some good news in this, and that
> of course is the departure and failure to
> return of Annette. Nobody wants Annette
> back, so it may turn out for the best.

Daddy wants Annette back, I thought. And I knew that I
wanted Annette back too, but I wasn't ready to say so. Especially to Joanna. I had planned to e-mail Marley and Bev and
Kelsey, but I didn't stay online. I went downstairs and joined
Angus for a few repetitions of the rain dance.

He was now taping the sound track of his videotape onto
a cassette tape for his battery-operated radio. This was not a
happy thought. A portable rain dance could quite easily become yet more portable public humiliation. I went down to
the dock and sat with Daddy. It was drizzling now, but still
hot out, and getting rained on in the heat is kind of fun.
"When is Annette coming back?"

"She's about ten miles away, but I think her pace is slowing. She can probably hear the rain dance from where she
is." My father smiled at me. "I was proud of you last night,
sweetie. Angus was a bum, but you kept your head."

"No, I didn't. I fell asleep. It was DeWitt who kept his
head."

"Nice kid," my father observed.

I had spent four weeks puttering around with DeWitt and
hadn't really seen him. But after we found Angus, DeWitt

put his arm around my shoulder and left it there, not a touch, but a weight. "I'm the hero," he told me contentedly. "I always wanted to be the hero."

I studied him. Thin cheeks and sharp, aggressive chin, brown eyes beneath heavy brows, a grin that spread his narrow cheeks so that they fit his wide forehead after all. He smelled of coconut from his suntan oil. I usually showered off my oils and lotions before I went to bed, but DeWitt hadn't, and although I had seen him in a bathing suit plenty of times, the thought passed through my mind that he would be wearing less in the shower, and all of a sudden I was out of breath and had to step away.

"He is nice," I agreed with Dad.

Rain dance music filled the air. Angus had climbed up onto the roof of the boathouse, where he was appealing to the gods of Vermont for water to combat a drought we were not having in the first place. The gods of Vermont must have found this irritating, because during a particularly frenzied period of stomping, Angus went through the roof. "Aaaaaagh!" he screamed. "My leg is broken!"

Daddy and I came running. He had actually gone only partway through the roof. Daddy grabbed the ladder that hangs lengthwise inside the boathouse. DeWitt told me once that it's to save people with in winter when they fall through the ice and you need to distribute your own weight safely on the thin ice from which you will rescue them, so

57

you slide out on the ladder and pull your drowning victim out of the frigid water. I didn't want to try it.

I was extremely jealous of Angus. All my life I have wanted a cast so I could be on crutches and hobble weakly and have my books carried by other people and be an object of attention and get funny signatures all up and down my plaster. The only consolation was that it was still summer. With any luck, Angus would have the cast off before school started and would thus gain no benefit from having gone through the boathouse roof.

However, once Daddy (on the roof) and I (inside the boathouse on the ladder) had pushed him all the way through, like Winnie-the-Pooh being shoved through Rabbit's hole by Christopher Robin, it turned out that all Angus needed was a Band-Aid.

"It rained, though," said Angus proudly.

"It was already raining!" hollered Daddy.

Angus felt this was a mere detail, hardly worth notice. We looked up to find Annette standing there, looking at us. "I don't want to know," she said. It wasn't a voice we'd heard her use before. Angus asked for permission to visit his bomb shelter for a few hours. It was granted. He probably could have gotten permission to live there permanently.

Daddy and Annette went inside the house. You could tell that they had serious things to discuss, and that you did not want to be part of it until you absolutely had to be. With excellent timing, as if he'd been watching through his binoculars, DeWitt rowed over to rescue me. I clambered into his boat, and he pushed off again. We weren't ten feet from my dock when he said, "Well? Who is Toby?"

"Toby?" I said.

"You did ask your father, didn't you?"

DeWitt pulled in the oars and rested them in the bottom of the boat. Now that his hands were free, he put them on my knees. I was wearing baggy shorts in gaudy yellow and orange, and a white T-shirt with alternating rows of tiny green trees and tiny red print saying christmasinvermontchristmasinvermont and so forth. I was smeared with lots of sun-protection lotion, and I had on a new pair of sunglasses with leopard-print frames. I felt mismatched, which was bad, but disguised, which was good.

"Well?" said DeWitt when we had gotten out to the middle of the lake.

"Well what?"

"Does he?"

"Does he what?"

"Does your father have another son?"

"Oh. I forgot to ask."

"How could you forget to ask your own father about the possibility of your own brother existing out there in a family that's not your own?" yelled DeWitt.

"Shhh! Don't yell! Sound carries."

59

"Your problem is you don't yell enough, Shelley. You ought to be yelling at Angus and yelling at your father and yelling at Joanna and yelling and yelling and yelling!" DeWitt's hands on my kneecaps tightened, and he shook me, the way you shake people by the shoulders. It made the tiny boat rock, and we both laughed.

"I really did forget," I said. "I'm sorry you reminded me. What if it's true? Because if it's true, Daddy abandoned that son."

DeWitt felt that knowing the facts would make it possible to deal with them. In his family, they always made sure to set forth the facts thoroughly and carefully prior to continuing discussions. I didn't admit that my family was neither thorough nor careful. "The facts of my family are hard enough without adding more of them," I said to DeWitt. "Anyway, if there is a Toby, then my father is a bad person, the kind of father whose black-and-white photograph hangs in post offices. Wanted: For Failure to Pay Child Support."

"You don't know that he didn't pay," said DeWitt. "You just know that he didn't have Toby at your house for any well-known holidays. But it does seem to me, speaking of course as just an outsider, that your father has made more than his share of major errors. I think—"

"He has not!" I yelled, thus satisfying at least one of DeWitt's requirements. I jumped up to get rid of DeWitt's hands on my knees, and DeWitt jumped up to emphasize his point, and New Yorkers that we are, we forgot about being in a very small boat, and we flipped.

It's an effective way to get somebody's hands off your knees. We sank into the icy-cold water—because a northern Vermont lake is not toasty even in July—and came up sputtering and casting blame on each other, especially over my sunglasses, which were now trout property. Then we had to right the boat, which was hard, and get our two bodies back in, which was the most embarrassing exhibition of bad coordination in Vermont that year, and then bail it out and also rescue the oars.

"I guess that's what it is to be unstable," said DeWitt, grinning. Lake water ran off his hair, got caught in his thick, wide eyebrows and became little brooks going down the sides of his cheeks. He looked different with his hair plastered down. Older and more interesting.

"I am not unstable," I said sharply. I took the oars myself to ensure that we would row to my dock and not to his.

DeWitt leaned back dramatically, locking his hands behind his head to make himself a pillow. He stared up at the sky as if he were a young intellectual at an English university, punting down the river. I was very proud of my rowing. I also kind of liked the way my wet T-shirt fit. We reached our dock, and I handed him the oars and stepped out onto the splintery gray wood.

"When you get back from your family reunion," he said, "I won't be here. We're going camping for a week, my grandfather and my father and I. We're hiking part of the Appalachian Trail, and then we all head on home to the city."

I was stunned. "You—you won't be here?" I whispered. "I—I won't see you again?"

DeWitt grinned so broadly his mouth seemed to curl around to his ears. He stuck an oar into the air, like the recipient of an athletic trophy, and yelled, "You're going to miss me!" using the singsong tune of "I've got a secret."

He rowed off backward, singing as loudly as an opera star. "She's going to miss me. She's going to miss me."

Lake people on porches, docks and boats applauded.

Oh, he was as embarrassing in public as Angus. It had just taken him longer to show his true colors. I stomped up to the house and slammed the screened door behind me.

Annette was preoccupied with Granger Elliott's job offer. You could see her weigh the pros and cons, tilting from one side to the other, studying an invisible balance sheet in her palm.

Daddy had been equally preoccupied by the job offer. Over and over he said he had not married Annette to acquire an at-home mother for his children. He had married her because he loved her. Still and all, if she took the regular job, he too would have to take a regular job, because he was traveling a lot, and now our actual mother was too far away to pitch in for a sick kid or whatever. It was okay, he said quickly, but it had to be thought through.

So what with all these things to settle and think through, Daddy didn't drive back to Montreal, and he didn't drive back to New York either. He fixed the boathouse roof. He removed the bomb shelter door permanently. He took all 1958 soup cans to the dump. He circled Annette, watched her warily from across the room and took her out for dinner and said he really, really loved the blue and yellow fabric, even though my father has never had a cloth thought in his life.

I called Marley and Bev and Kelsey, and I meant to tell them everything, but I didn't. I listened instead. Marley had a maybe boyfriend. Bev had a maybe job as a model. Kelsey had a definite boyfriend. It was terrible to be a mere listener. Everything I had to say stuck in my throat. I didn't share my maybe summer boyfriend, DeWitt, and I didn't share my maybe brother, Toby, and I didn't share my maybe half-gone stepmother. I could hear, but not talk. They were my best friends—but something (geography? loyalty?) kept me from confiding.

Grandma called from Arizona. She too was on her way to Barrington. She had wonderful presents for us and a new digital video camera and lots of things we could only guess at. Angus and I tried to guess anyway. We love presents.

Aunt Maggie called for last-minute plane arrival details and said she had made enough potato salad to drown in, and also lime Jell-O with shredded carrots in it, and shortcake for strawberries, and homemade peach ice cream. Angus didn't even tell her he would die before eating lime green Jell-O with shredded carrots in it. He requested that a pint, possibly two, of the peach ice cream be reserved for him personally.

The reunion started to feel possible and maybe even fun. I planned things to do with my cousin Carolyn, and secrets to tell. I got stranded on those secrets, like a swimmer at low tide, thinking of the secret that might or might not exist.

And then Daddy dropped a little bomb of his own.

Not the Toby bomb.

"The company has scheduled a retreat," he said. "I have no choice. I have to go. My career's on the line. So I have to miss the start of the family reunion. You three will go on without me. I'll catch up later."

He beamed at us hopefully, as if he were Angus's age, a twelve-year-old hoping a big, wide smile under red hair and freckled nose would make everything okay.

Annette didn't yell at Daddy for abandoning her to the clutches of the in-laws she hardly knew, and she didn't yell at Angus for causing all this, and she didn't yell at me for standing around doing nothing. She just sagged.

I could not bear it if she got all saggy when we met the Perfects. She had turned out pretty decent there for a while. I wanted to put her on display, like a new car; let them drive her around a little, admire the paint job, try out the accessories, and agree that Daddy had done all right for himself after all.

But he hadn't. And he was abandoning her, and us, to face his family reunion without him. Was he ashamed of her? Of us? Or would Celeste really be there, and he couldn't handle it?

Or would Toby be there, and he *really* couldn't handle that?

Chapter Six

"What is this?" demanded the security guard, although any-body could see that it was a leg. She peered down the hollow leg, squinting, as if finding some distant horizon down toward the knee.

"It's my brother's leg," I said.

The leg was long, curvy and slim, with red-painted toe-nails. "Your brother's leg," she repeated.

"I'm just holding it for him," I explained.

Annette pretended to be having purse problems. She shuffled through credit cards and debit cards and receipts and pencils without tips. She has one of those bottomless-pit handbags, almost a suitcase, that holds her entire life and part of ours. It matches nothing, so no matter what Annette wears and how good she looks, the outfit falls apart the minute she hoists that handbag. She located a lipstick. Annette loves to buy new lipstick, and previous lipsticks gather at the bottom of her purse, adding weight and substance. She was currently using Tiger Eye. Of course if your tiger actually had eyes that color, you would know it had a dreaded infection.

They searched me thoroughly, including my shoes. I hoped they would search Angus twice as thoroughly, since it was his leg.

Angus raced up, waving a poster he had bought in the airport gift shop. "I can keep it from getting wrinkled by stuffing it down my leg," he said happily.

Four security guards considered this possibility. "What exactly is the leg for?" asked one of them.

"Annoying my cousins," said Angus.

They nodded. "Should work." They put it through the X ray, to make sure it wasn't carrying lethal instruments. I decided it was not the time to describe Angus as a lethal instrument, although I was closing in on that opinion. Angus begged and pleaded to be searched, including all body cavities, but the guards, like others in Angus's life, had already tired of him and waved him through.

"These are your children?" they asked Annette.

"Stepchildren," she said quickly. She was wearing a white

cotton dress of the Indian sort—a million gathers of pre-wrinkled gauze. It had begun its life limp; now in the heat of August it was limper, and by the time we got off the plane it would be limpest. Her necklace had twisted so that the clasp and not the pendant hung in front. Her hair was collecting in her face.

She did not look like a wicked stepmother, but a whipped one.

Incredibly, they let us on board with the leg.

It was a huge plane. We were in the center of a row with five seats across, and none of us had an aisle seat. The leg did not fit beneath the seat in front of Angus. The luggage compartments over our heads were already full, but Angus stood on tiptoe on his seat and made an effort to rearrange other people's stuff and jam his leg into the space. Shoving at the plaster toes, he muttered to himself that people had awfully big suitcases these days.

The businesswoman sitting on the aisle between Angus and freedom closed her eyes and steeled herself for a long ride. When the flight attendant returned, the businesswoman asked if there were any open seats she could move to.

"No," said the flight attendant, deeply sympathetic, "but at least I can put the leg in the garment-bag closet up front. Little boy, may I take that for you?"

Angus handed it over silently. In his hands, the leg looked

comical, but when the flight attendant held it up against her trim little uniform and crisp little scarf and perky little hair, the leg was a body part, as if detectives would shortly find a torso and skull under other seats. Angus sank back against the cushions and buckled his seat belt. "I shouldn't have brought it," he whispered to me. After a long time, he said, "I shouldn't have brought my collections either."

He had packed a whole suitcase full of stuff he planned to show off to Brett. I could not imagine the sixteen-year-old who would waste time on Angus's junk. I was relieved that we were going to keep Angus's crazy treasures a secret. Then, very softly, he whispered, "I don't actually care if the Perfects laugh at me. I don't actually mind if they think I'm a jerk. But they're going to laugh at Annette, aren't they?"

"I don't think they'll laugh at her in front of us," I whispered back. "The thing is, Angus, since Daddy isn't here, we have to take his place. We have to be Annette's protection."

Angus moaned softly.

"What's the matter?" asked Annette.

"Ummmm," said Angus, who is an excellent liar, but was derailed at the moment. "I was thinking of my suitcase of stuff. I shouldn't have brought it. I should have brought clothes, like you suggested. Maybe I'll just abandon it at the baggage claim."

"Then the airport police would come after us," said Annette. "I just barely didn't get arrested for child abuse when

I left you guys with the neighbors. What would happen to me if I started abandoning heavy items at airports? Suitcases whose contents cannot be explained by normal persons?"

The businesswoman on the aisle shuddered. We had already been judged and found lacking. It was easy to imagine how the Perfects would see us.

Annette got out her cross-stitch. She loves embroidery. She is forever making authentic Early American samplers to frame in dark wood and hang all over our walls. Wherever you turn, there is a little piece of reading material that will make you a better person and let you see a row of tulips and hearts as well. But during the entire flight, Annette never even got around to threading her needle. She just sat staring at the little cross-stitch cottage, with its little cross-stitch roof and its tidy cross-stitch trees. I thought it was probably the life she had expected to live: all lined up and facing the right way.

Angus, who loves airline food and often patrols the aisle asking innocent passengers if he can have their little packs of salted nuts, sat motionless. He didn't talk. I would not have said Angus was capable of silence.

All that silence gave me time to wrestle with what was coming. Joanna had called up late the night before on my phone, not the family phone, so I had not felt obligated to tell anybody about it. "I'm coming after all!" she cried. "Isn't that wonderful? Aren't you thrilled? You guys were having such a great summer, and I'm stuck here and I'm tired of Jean-Paul and France, and I never want to do anything again that starts with the letter *c* like castles or cathedrals or concerts or culture. So I'll be there in two days."

I don't want you, I thought. If you come, you'll be the one who's friends with Carolyn and goes places with Brett and finds out about Toby and stays up with the grown-ups sharing high school memories. You'll be in front of me, in charge of me, older than me, more interesting than me. "That's great, Jo," I said.

What an awful age fourteen is: Everybody changing shape, like summer becoming fall. The shape of my body was changing without my permission, but the shock was the changing shape of my family. I never gave anybody permission to change my parents, my address and my life. And now, equally without my permission, the posture of my love for Joanna had changed.

Am I growing up, I thought, or just growing mean?

"I've got the most wonderful clothes now," said Joanna smugly. "Wait till you see; you'll die. You can borrow anything, though, because I have so much."

She's going to be Perfect, too, I thought. She'll be part of them, not us.

"I'll take charge, Shelley," said my sister confidently. "We'll push Annette into a corner and let her fade there."

When Joanna had flown to Paris, on the day school ended in early June, Annette had still been an interloper.

But since then, we had dealt with bomb shelter time-shares. Gone for bagels in Boston. Paraded hollow legs around town. Sold zinnias by leaping in front of cars. We were almost—well, within a mountain range or two—a family.

"Annette's not so bad," I said.

Joanna laughed scornfully. "What—is she listening?" said my sister.

What if, when we got to Barrington, Joanna was the interloper in our family? Somebody who lopes around, getting in between you and what you care about. If she didn't get between me and anything else, Joanna would certainly get between me and attention. How could my summer hold a candle to hers? Even my sunglasses weren't going to measure up to hers.

I knew then that nobody would squeeze lemons for lemonade. They would dump imitation lemonade powder into a Tupperware jug and swish it around and toss it over ice cubes, and it wouldn't count.

The plane landed.

It was so bumpy a landing that the whole plane held its breath and exhaled in unison once we were definitely down. My hands had gone cold. We shuffled out of the plane into the red-carpeted arm of the terminal. I hate those portable folding hallways. I feel as if I'm in a vacuum cleaner, about to be sucked up into something suffocating.

"Is my hair all right?" whispered Annette.

Her hair looked awful. "You look great, Annette," I told her.

She got out her purse mirror to check. "I look terrible. You were being kind. You know you've touched bottom when a stepchild is kind."

"There they are!" shouted Angus, running ahead. Whatever had silenced him during the flight had evaporated.

The Perfects were in a row, neatly arranged by height, just as I had remembered them. Grandma was the shortest, her hair whiter and thinner. She beamed and held out her arms for Angus. Aunt Maggie was next, streaky blond and beautiful in sleek white trousers with a crisp navy top and polka-dotted accessories and fragile sandals. Uncle Todd was in khaki pants, a safari shirt and sneakers so white he must have bought them an hour before. Carolyn was taller than her father, looking cool and calm and only slightly interested. She raised an eyebrow as Angus whooped and hollered and flung himself on his relatives.

I'm afraid, I thought. It's like school. It's a test. We're Perfect—are you? What's your score? Where do you rank? Our expectations are low.

I will be Perfect, I told myself. I will make Annette Perfect. I will kill anybody who implies by a single syllable that Daddy is anything other than Perfect. When my Perfect sister arrives, I will Perfectly defer to her.

I advanced smoothly, as if on wheels. This would set the pace for our whole visit.

"Wait!" cried the flight attendant. She raced up to me. "You forgot your leg!" she shouted, thrusting it into my arms.

Chapter Seven

Uncle Todd and Angus were in the workshop off the three-car garage, drilling, because Uncle Todd said the leg would be easier to carry around if it had a rope sling.

"Like a submachine gun!" said Angus happily. "Just casually thrown over my shoulder."

Uncle Todd's approval of everything Angus was and said and had brought on the plane had restored Angus's spirits. It had not done the same for Annette. "I'm going to carry a lifelong grudge against that flight attendant," Annette said to me.

Aunt Maggie said primly, "Perhaps Angus should not have been permitted to bring the leg to start with. I can well imagine that Charlie would have been entertained by it, however. My brother always likes to draw attention to himself. That's why I know he will love this weekend. When is his flight getting in?"

Annette looked vague.

Great, I thought. Wife Number Three has no idea when husband's flight arrives. We're talking seriously Not Perfect here. "Why?" I said brightly. "Do you have something planned, Aunt Maggie? Here. Let me help carry the glasses and drinks outside."

But Carolyn and Aunt Maggie had this under control, of course, and we headed for the backyard, which was nothing like I remembered. Gone was the torn, sagging badminton net, replaced by a long, slim lap pool with blue tiles and yellow stripes underwater. Gone was the patchy grass, replaced by lovely decks and well-planned stretches of brick. Gone were the holes dug by the neighbor's dog. Now everything was edged by impressive gardens, where flowers stood tall and bloomed bright.

Carolyn poured iced tea into frosted glasses, adding slices of lemon and passing a tiny plate of tiny cookies, which probably had a tiny amount of flavor. I happen to detest iced tea. You can add sugar for days and still not have a drink worth pouring down your throat.

We sat beneath a yellow awning, gazing at the towering oaks around us while a single fluffy cloud nicely punctuated a blue sky. The poolside furniture was sleek and sophisticated. The house itself had central air now, so the hummy sound of window units and ceiling fans was just another memory, soft and vibrating in my past. "No swings?" I said sadly. "No hammock and sandbox?"

Carolyn and Aunt Maggie laughed. "We got rid of those years ago," said my aunt. "Children of divorce, I notice," she informed Annette, "always yearn for the safer, more controlled parts of their childhood."

Annette squeezed a little acid from her lemon into her iced tea.

Grandma said, "I think I'll lie down for a while. I nap every day now. It was such a long drive from the airport. But wake me up the minute Charlie arrives."

I laughed. "It'll be a long nap, Grandma," I told her. "He's not coming till Wednesday."

"What?" shrieked Aunt Maggie. "What do you mean, he's not coming till Wednesday? The party is tomorrow night! Saturday night!" She was so upset that she leaped right out of her chair. The chairs had beautiful cushions, the kind you take inside every night, because they'd be ruined by rain. In our family, we would just use them ruined, but no doubt the Perfects never forgot the task of cushion retrieval.

Annette said nervously, "I know. I'm so sorry. Your twentieth anniversary is such a milestone. It's such an important date. He's so sorry he's missing it. But he doesn't think you'll notice he's not here. He picked out a gift for you and Todd. I have it in my bag, and when he gets here on Wednesday, he's planning of course to take you out to dinner to celebrate, and of course—"

"He said he would be here for the weekend!" Aunt Maggie screamed.

Annette and I looked at each other.

My aunt flopped back down into her chair. She looked even more limp than Annette. She began to cry. "It isn't our twentieth anniversary," she said. "I mean, it is, but that's not the party. The party is for Charlie. I put together a huge surprise party for him. People are flying in from all over the country. I have all our old high school friends coming. I have a caterer and a band and a million rented chairs and table-cloths."

"Oh, dear," said Grandma. "Well, that's the problem with surprise parties, isn't it? The main character doesn't know that he should schedule it."

"You get on the phone, Annette," cried Aunt Maggie, "and explain to him that he is coming. He's to cancel everything and get here in a timely fashion!"

Annette had rarely looked so incompetent. It was unimaginable that Granger Elliott would want this woman back. It seemed more likely that he had thrown a party when she left. She spilled her tea on her dress and stared hopelessly at the stain it would certainly leave. "Actually, I don't actually have a way to reach him right now," she said, which was a meaningless remark, because he was never without his cell phone.

"He's on a company retreat," said Annette. "They're bonding. He has to be there. It's the new chairman of the board and the new chief financial officer, and he's experiencing the wilderness together with them, and it's crucial to his career."

This sounded so unlike my father that I started giggling. He would probably bond by helping the others escape their wilderness duties, and he'd find a wide-screen television on which to watch a really good baseball game while surrounded by really good food.

"A wilderness retreat," Aunt Maggie repeated, in the same tone of voice she no doubt had used behind our backs to say, "That boy brought a leg." Still crying, she said, "It's just like Charlie to do this to me. I invited his favorite teachers! His coaches! Our old neighbors who used to say Charlie was going to meet some terrible doom! And he isn't going to show up?" Aunt Maggie looked surprisingly like Joanna. She pouted in the same way, lips puffed out on the bottom and tucked in at the top. "I should have known Charlie would vanish when I need him. Charlie is never there when you count on him."

I stopped trying to be polite about her nasty cold tea and

poured it out into the grass. "Daddy's always there when *we* count on him," I said.

"Shelley, you don't have to defend him to me. I understand your father all too well."

Now Carolyn took up the slack, listing the effort that had gone into making this a special occasion. Locating friends not heard from in twenty years. Finding overnight housing for all these friends. Ninety-seven friends, to be exact.

"Ninety-seven friends?" said Annette, dumbfounded. "I thought his whole high school graduating class had only fifty-five in it."

"I'm including spouses, of course," said Aunt Maggie. "Plenty of our guests are strangers to me, married to our dear old friends. They'll have been listening to Charlie stories for years. And now he won't be here!"

Ninety-seven people with gifts and expectations, and I would have to make excuses for my father.

I imagined a reunion of Angus's friends twenty or thirty years from now. There would most certainly be ninety-seven of those, and they too would have been telling Angus stories for years. But if there were any Shelley stories worth remembering for two decades, I couldn't think of them.

Grandma kissed Aunt Maggie. "You'll have to make the best of it, dear. You've always been able to make the best of things. I know you can triumph over this." She went off for her nap, and I thought she might possibly sleep for several days, skipping Wednesday, so as to avoid being there when Aunt Maggie had a chance to tell Daddy what she thought of him.

"Where's Brett?" I said brightly, because we were in need of a subject change, and no doubt Brett was off doing something impressive that needed bragging about.

"He'll be around later," said Carolyn. "Let's swim. Who wants to swim?"

There seemed to be very little interest in swimming. If Aunt Maggie acts like Joanna as well as looks like Joanna, I thought, then I know what will happen now. She'll forget what she's mad about and get stranded inside her frown and stare about in a confused sort of way. This was one of Joanna's nicest traits. Angus was always capitalizing upon it. "Swimming," said Aunt Maggie, looking confused. "Yes, of course. Carolyn, tell Shelley all about your swimming awards."

"Mom, she's not interested in that," said Carolyn uncomfortably. "Let's talk about Joanna's summer in Paris instead."

It might not be the right time to mention that Joanna was bailing on Paris and would be in Barrington on Sunday. The Perfects were looking at another very long drive to the airport the day after their failed party, and then a third drive when Daddy finally landed. Maybe Daddy would have the sense to rent a car. It was only fair to let the Perfects know that Joanna was coming, but on the other hand, Annette didn't know either, and there was only so much evidence of sloppy stepmothering I wanted on hand.

"Oh, Joanna hasn't done anything except visit cathedrals and castles," I said. "Whereas Angus sold time-shares in a bomb shelter and almost became a millionaire."

Aunt Maggie was not amused. "Surely this sort of sick prank could have been prevented. Is it wise, do you think, for Charlie to be away so much?"

Annette said she thought it was wise for him to earn a living.

Aunt Maggie said she was worried about how the children were turning out, scattered around the world before we were even out of our teens.

I knew the next sentence would include the word *stability*, so once again I changed the subject. "Annette is thinking of going back to work."

Aunt Maggie was appalled. Not only did we have to have a stepmother, the woman had hardly arrived before she was running off.

Carolyn said, "I'm going to take Shelley to the pool, Mom. See you later. Bye, Annette." She stood up. I did too, although since we weren't two feet away from the pool, I wasn't sure why we needed to say good-bye.

"We put in this beautiful pool," said Aunt Maggie, jiggling her glass to make the ice cubes dance, "but you know how contrary the young are. Still hanging out at the town pool instead of using this one." She tried to laugh, but her heart wasn't in it.

Proving her desperation, Annette said, "And what's happening these days on the school board, Maggie?"

"We're debating whether to add another wing to the middle school or send the eighth grade over to the high school, where there's space. I'm very, very, very opposed to having the eighth grade in the same building as the high school students."

"Oh," said Annette sympathetically. "Are the teenagers here in Barrington all on drugs or something? You have to shelter the little ones from their older brothers and sisters? What a shame."

I decided Annette was going to be fine.

Carolyn and I went into the house to change into bathing suits. I was to sleep in her room, and Angus in Brett's, while Grandma had the guest room. Annette was sleeping on the sofa bed in the huge family room, where Daddy would join her on Wednesday. "Where is Brett anyway?" I asked Carolyn.

"We'll see him tonight at a Little League game. He's a coach."

Her room was extremely neat. Everything was folded or rolled or stacked. All colors matched. All photos were in frames. "Do you like your stepmother?" she said.

I don't like that word. She's not my mother. As for step, it sounds as if we're walking on her. "You mean Annette?" I said.

Carolyn giggled. "You have more stepmothers I don't know about? That sounds like Uncle Charlie."

My throat got hot and tight, and my contact lenses scraped my eyes. I wiggled into my bathing suit and pulled my jeans up over it. I considered heading back to Annette and pulling the plug on this whole family reunion nightmare. If I said, "Annette, we're out of here," she'd rent a car and throw Angus in the back, and we'd head for Disney World instead.

Carolyn wanted to know if I knew how to ride a bike, since she realized that I had grown up in New York City, where it was impossible to have a bike. Actually bikes are everywhere in New York, but I skipped this and reminded Carolyn that her own father had taught me how to ride a bike in her own driveway. "Didn't your parents have time?" said Carolyn kindly.

We cycled past lawns green from sprinklers and under trees so tall and leafy they made tunnels over the street. We turned right at the old brick elementary school, which had the shuttered look of schools over summer: hot and dusty, books waiting, chairs stacked. In the distance spread farms. Past the reach of sprinklers, the color of Barrington in August was not green. The color was sunburn, everything toasted. A field far off was like melted butter. Dust rose from highways.

At the pool, Carolyn bought us hot dogs and fries from the concession. She slathered hers with ketchup, and I whitened mine with salt, and we joined her friends. I got that sick, tight feeling that happens when strangers inspect you. It was clear that none of her friends swam. They decorated the pool rim, they tanned and they wore bathing suits, but they didn't swim.

Carolyn surprised me. "This," she said proudly, as if I were a fashion model on the runway, spotlights casting mysterious shadows over my high cheekbones, "is my cousin Shelley."

"Oh, yes," said one of the friends, tapping her teeth with the earpiece of her sunglasses, "you're the one whose father had to leave Barrington, didn't he?"

She smiled. She had small pointy teeth, like a baby's. Her hair was extremely thin and straight. Her eyes were bright and gloating. She knew something I didn't know.

"Give it a rest, Miranda," said Carolyn. "Want to play tennis, Shelley?"

I don't know how to play tennis. I'm not a great swimmer either, but I needed distance, so I said, "I think I'll swim while you play tennis."

The water was warm from the sun, and it helped me keep my temper. It did nothing to calm my fear. My father had to leave Barrington? What did that mean?

I swam slowly to the far end of the pool and got out on the opposite side and sat on the edge, my feet in the water. Travel is so strange. We'd left Vermont before breakfast and arrived in Barrington in midafternoon, yet my life did not feel hundreds of miles away. It felt hundreds of years away. My father seemed so distant, he might actually be the person Aunt Maggie said he was, never there when you counted on him.

A bunch of boys charged out of the dressing rooms. I graded them according to Joanna's system. A definite ten, a nine and the rest eights. Barrington knew how to do boys. Joanna would have a great visit. The boys drew closer, and instead of taking advantage of this fine perspective, I glanced down at my knees. Last year we had to take health class. The teacher skipped quickly over tough health subjects (sex, AIDS, pregnancy) and went straight to an easy health subject: relationships.

The whole curriculum was designed to ruin me. "Children of divorce," the teacher told us frequently, "especially if it is the mother who has abandoned them, have a poor self-image. They fear affection. They shrink from love."

Mother abandoned Daddy, that's true. But she didn't abandon us. The first two years, she and Jean-Paul lived two blocks away and we saw her all the time, and she did homework with Angus and shopping with Joanna and giggling with me. Then, when Jean-Paul had to go back to France—even then she wasn't abandoning us. It was just that she couldn't have Jean-Paul and us too.

I didn't explain this to the health teacher. In fact I got a low grade in that class. "Not participating," wrote the teacher, for whom silence was not a virtue. But the truth is, I remember everything she said better than Shakespeare or the Preamble to the Constitution. Sometimes when I am very sad and the blankets on my bed aren't heavy enough or warm enough or cozy enough, I think, *She did abandon us.*

One of the boys sat down next to me. The nine. Very tan, the hairs on his chest sun-bleached gold. His face was slathered with sun protection he hadn't rubbed in enough, and his sunglasses had slid down to the tip of his slippery nose, and I looked straight into his eyes. My hair was drying fast in the heat, and its damp corkscrews brushed against his arm, he was sitting so close.

"Hi there," he said. "You must be Carolyn's cousin." His voice was deep and scratchy, as if he needed to clear his throat. Had Carolyn pointed me out? Or did everyone in Barrington really and truly know everyone else, and I was the only stranger in town?

I nodded. "My brother's here too."

"Hey, great. I'm, um, coming to the party tomorrow night. For your, um, dad. Looking forward to meeting everybody." He pushed his sunglasses up and hid his eyes.

"He won't be there," I said. "Aunt Maggie planned the party without consulting us, and my father isn't coming till next week."

"Oh, no!" The boy burst into laughter. "That sounds just

like Mrs. Preffyn. I've tangled with her. So it's just you and your brother?"

"And my father's wife. Annette."

He took the sunglasses off and looked intently at me.

I was abruptly, wildly, crazily, intensely attracted to him. I was aware of my new parrot-colored bathing suit and how it fit. I was aware of his baggy trunks and how they fit. I was breathless and happy and scared.

Like Joanna, would I now see each boy the way a grocery shopper sees peaches? This one isn't ripe; this one has a bruise; this one is perfect—I'll take it!

"You have stepbrothers or stepsisters?" he asked.

"No. Thank goodness. It's hard enough taking on a stepmother." I told him about Angus—bomb shelter, leg, rain dance and all.

"He sounds terrific," said the boy. "I can't wait to meet him. I don't have the kind of personality that can take on stuff like that."

"Few do," I said. "For which we can all be grateful."

We laughed together. I was resting part of my weight on my hand, which was spread open on the wet pool tiles. His hand was doing the same, and there was perhaps half an inch of space between our fingertips. I considered crossing the distance and touching his hand. Maybe this was love at first sight. If so, every sacrifice made was going to be worth it.

Carolyn trotted up. She knelt down between us. "Hi, Toby," she said. "Thanks for baby-sitting the cousin for me."

Chapter Eight

The cousin.

Sometimes you hear men refer to their wives like that. *The* wife. I hate that.

What I needed to know was, was this *the* Toby?

Who knew the answer? Who wouldn't smirk when I asked? Who wouldn't give me a list of things my father had done wrong? Who would give me the answer I wanted, which was that Angus had made up his Toby, and this Toby—another Toby entirely—sat beside me because he thought I looked interesting, and possibly pretty. He was not related to me.

But Toby, whoever he was, vanished with his friends while Carolyn and I pedaled home to change clothes and help with dinner, although Aunt Maggie was so organized there was nothing to help with. Annette and I sat by the pool while Carolyn prepared for our picnic.

First she covered the large redwood table with a scarlet cotton cloth that had weights sewn in the corners so it wouldn't blow away. Then she took four white runners, which she thumbtacked right down into the table, making eight place mats. Horizontally down the center, creating a plaid, she tacked a narrow, brilliant blue ribbon. The table setting was pretty and patriotic, but more like something a kindergartner would design than Carolyn, who seemed eager to be sophisticated.

The words of my sophisticated sister, Joanna, ran through my mind. *I always used to think that Daddy and Celeste had a son they never told us about, and somehow I would meet him, all unaware . . .*

The person with whom I could have shared my thoughts right now was DeWitt, the only one who possessed all the background information. But I couldn't even e-mail him, with that safe, enclosed feeling e-mail has, because e-mail isn't safe or enclosed, and anyway, he was off hiking and almost certainly was not backpacking e-mail access.

At that moment, as Carolyn patted the picnic table, the loss of DeWitt, whom I scarcely knew, was as dreadful and piercing as the loss of my mother.

"I thought of this color scheme," said Carolyn proudly, as if she personally had invented red, white and blue. "When I was really little. Ever since, we've done every single picnic just the same way. I used to color in the white paper napkins with my own designs, but I don't anymore." She held up large white cloth napkins, on which a child's lopsided, madly grinning crayon figures had been embroidered. "Mother immortalized some of my masterpieces," said Carolyn, laughing.

My eyes got misty. We don't have family traditions from when I was little. After Mother left, nobody felt like keeping anything going, and Annette hasn't started any new ones. Besides, once you're as old as I am, it's too late.

Carolyn went back into the kitchen. Annette walked over to the table and picked up an embroidered napkin and fingered it. "That is so sweet. When I have a baby, I'm going to do everything like that, too."

I practically fainted. "When you have a baby? Are you—I mean—you and Daddy—you're—"

"No," said Annette sharply, "and don't start any rumors. But I might. Someday. I love kids."

I thought this was very brave of her, considering what the three kids she knew best had subjected her to for the last year and a half.

But it was too much. Too many people, too much coming and going, too many contrasts, too many worries. I felt the way I had when I was eleven and the divorce was happening; when both my parents were both right and wrong, and we loved them and hated them too; when sleep was never restful and meals never peaceful.

My grandmother came slowly into the yard and lowered herself onto a pile of cushions. I poured her a glass of tea, and she held it against her cheek, already overheated.

Angus raced into the yard brandishing a tennis racket. "Uncle Todd is teaching me how to play!" he shouted. "Uncle Todd says I'm a natural. Uncle Todd says I'm probably going to be a tennis star pretty soon." Angus swatted invisible tennis balls with great vigor.

The balls felt real, bouncing off me, bruising me.

"Shelley, darling, are you all right?" said my grandmother. "It's the heat, isn't it? Barrington is such a furnace in August. Civilized people can hardly survive backyards in August. Come sit in the shade with me, sweetie. You and I haven't had a chance to talk yet. You must tell me everything."

I made myself skinny so I could lie on the chaise lounge next to Grandma. Even in the fierce heat it was wonderful to snuggle and be soothed. Grandma said a person couldn't be too careful in the sun, and I looked a little pink to her. She hoped I was not the kind of girl who obsessed about a tan, because too much sun was bad for lovely complexions like mine. When was I coming to visit her in Arizona? She had missed me so much.

It was pretty nice to have somebody worrying about me besides me.

Grandma took some of her own sun-protection lotion and began massaging it into my hands and up my arms. The veins in her hands stood out, knotted blue against age-spotted skin. Her knuckles were twisted, and her rings swung loosely on arthritis-curled fingers.

Grandma is old, I thought.

At the surprise party, everybody would say to Angus and to me, "My, how you've grown!" but they would say nothing to Grandma. You couldn't say, "My, how you've aged!"

I had no grandmother now laughing on her old front porch while our roller skates dented her floor. No more changes, I thought desperately. I can't face any more changes. Grandma is slowing down, but don't let her come to a full stop.

"Now, after supper," said Uncle Todd, flipping hamburgers on the grill, "we can't play tennis, Angus, because we'll be watching Brett's Little League team. He coaches Town and Country Gas."

"He what?" said Angus.

Carolyn gurgled with laughter. "The teams are named for their sponsors, who provide the uniforms and the ice cream afterward. We're very big on ice cream and T-shirts in Barrington. Win or lose, you get ice cream, you get a T-shirt. Tonight, Town and Country Gas is playing against Crest Septic Service. Those kids have a motto printed in maroon letters on their T-shirts: SEPTIC PUMPING IS BEST WITH CREST."

Angus was reverent. Nobody in New York would have a

T-shirt that said that. He wanted a T-shirt from Crest Septic Service.

"It won't be an exciting game," Carolyn warned us. She passed potato salad, and Angus, who hates mayonnaise, gagged. She passed deviled eggs, and Angus, who hates hard-boiled eggs, gagged. "Better fix me six or eight hamburgers," he told Uncle Todd. "There's nothing else to eat."

"Why won't the ball game be exciting?" Annette asked.

"Because they're only nine years old. If they even hit the ball, we stand up and cheer, but mostly they only get to base by being walked. I don't think there's any such thing as a really great nine-year-old pitcher."

We were eating and passing plates and not using our embroidered napkins, because they were too good to be used, when I realized that Grandma was filming us. I choked on my potato salad, and she laughed and put away the video camera. "The moment you're self-conscious, the film's no good," she said. "But think what pleasure I'll have next winter putting this in the VCR to play for myself and have a nice, warm and sunny my-family-is-the-best-in-the-world moment." She sat beside me, but it was difficult for her to swing her legs over the picnic-table bench. Uncle Todd held out a hand to guard her against falling.

"I'll film!" shouted Angus. He spent the rest of the meal taking close-ups of people chewing.

"Time for presents," announced Grandma. "You have to

eat lots and lots before you open presents, so you're stuffed and happy and ready. Then you rip off the ribbons and the paper and see your new treasures and top them off with cake and ice cream."

"My kind of schedule," said Angus.

Aunt Maggie filmed Angus opening his first. Videos, of course; old favorites—early James Bond, early Indiana Jones, early Star Wars, early Harry Potter. At least we wouldn't be subjected to the rain dance again. He also got a pogo stick, which he immediately hopped himself into the pool on and surfaced still bouncing at the shallow end. Finally, a tennis racket and two containers of neon yellow balls. "This is better than Christmas," said Angus, hanging up his pogo stick to dry and hugging Grandma fiercely, the way Daddy has taught us to hug. Squash the person.

"Easy," said Grandma, "I need my ribs intact." She wasn't joking. Some of Grandma had gone by, vanishing like the color of trees in autumn. She was closer to winter now, frail and easily broken.

"Gather round," Grandma told us. "Shelley's gift is small." She handed me a velvet box the size of my spread hand, and I opened the box's clasp, which was the shape of a princess's crown. Inside lay a necklace of gold lace with tendrils of seed pearls dangling from the gold and, at the center, one large pearl wrapped in a gold ribbon.

"It's beautiful!" I breathed. "Is it old?"

"It was your grandfather's engagement gift to me, Shelley," she said.

I could hardly remember my grandfather. I thought of them, all those years ago, young and in love, when such a necklace was just the right gift.

"But it isn't the kind of thing people need in retirement communities. I want you to have it. You'll be going to proms and dances, and this is a necklace for very special occasions."

"Shelley has just the neck for it," said Aunt Maggie. "Long and fashion-model."

"I'd have to have the perfect dress, though," I said, holding up the filigree of gold.

"Very, very low-cut," said Carolyn.

"Not that low-cut," said her mother.

"This will be such fun," said Annette, touching the lacy gold curlicue around the large pearl. "We'll spend months shopping for the perfect dress, Shelley. Promise me not to find the right dress the first afternoon we look."

I promised, although it seemed to me that even more crucial than the perfect dress was being asked to this dance by some perfect boy to start with. "Oh, Grandma!" I said. "Thank you so much. It's so lovely."

"Don't cry, darling," she said, holding me and the necklace close. But I cried anyhow, and for a horrible moment I thought everything painful might come out of me, in one great sob, but luckily Angus said, "Don't get mushy. Yuck."

"Girls do that," said Uncle Todd. "You get used to it. Come on, everybody, quick. We've got to get to the game."

Grandma stayed home, because she was tired, but the rest of us climbed into the huge, shiny SUV and headed for the baseball diamond behind the elementary school. Green-painted bleachers held parents, brothers and sisters. The sun was going down, the heat was tolerable and there was a nice breeze. All the little players hit their bats against the ground to make dust storms, and all the coaches squatted about, giving advice nobody listened to.

"Which is Brett?" I asked.

Carolyn pointed. "Blue-and-yellow baseball cap on backward. Come on, we'll sit with everybody else." She grabbed us two cans of soda from Aunt Maggie's canvas holdall and a pack of cupcakes.

I knew Annette did not want to be deserted, so I didn't meet her eyes as I deserted her. We clambered over the bleachers to the top row on the far side, where a dozen older kids sat in the shade of a huge oak. As we left, Annette was being introduced to somebody. "Oh, Charlie's latest wife!" said a cooing woman. "How sweet."

Miranda looked down at me from the top bleacher. "Oh, the cousin," said pointy-toothed Miranda. "How sweet."

Carolyn and I sat below Miranda, presumably to avoid looking at her nasty little face.

"Brett get his car back yet?" asked Miranda, poking her nose, which had the same profile as her teeth, into Carolyn's face.

"No," said Carolyn woodenly.

Miranda burst into a flutter of giggles, like pigeons on a sidewalk when you scuffle through them. "Your cousin Brett," she said, pointing her nose at me, "believes that anybody who obeys the rules of the road is just a coward. You should see Brett drive. Of course, you won't, because his father took away his car, and Brett moved out of the house and is living with Johnny Cameron, and of course the Perfect Preffyns aren't admitting that they have a sort of problem with their unperfect—"

"Shut up, Miranda," said Carolyn.

Miranda was not the shutting-up sort. "Brett was chalking up points by hitting old ladies, Seeing Eye dogs and toddlers in diapers," she told me gladly.

"He was not!" hissed Carolyn. "He took the corner too fast, his tires screeched and scared the old lady, and she stumbled on the curb and that's how she broke her ankle. Brett did not hit her. Nobody hit her. And Brett called the ambulance and went with her to the hospital. So there."

"Now you're saying that," said Miranda. "But at the police station, you were first in line to lynch your own brother, you were so mad at him for not being a Perfect Preffyn."

By now we had missed the first inning. I glanced at the

scoreboard. It didn't matter. Nobody had gotten on base, never mind made a run.

I could hardly wait to tell Annette about Brett. What ammunition. Not just a flaw, but a huge, gaping—

Midway between the grown-ups and us, alone on a middle bleacher, Angus was slowly wrapping himself in toilet paper. He had used half a roll, and both legs looked as if he had plaster casts. He was working on his left arm. He finished the arm and began on his forehead.

Carolyn was too busy defending a brother to notice. I have defended a brother in my time. It's humiliating and necessary, and you hate your brother for making you do it, and you'd hate yourself if you didn't.

"You say one more thing about Brett," said Carolyn, "and I'm going to sock you so hard you'll need dentures, Miranda."

I was filled with respect for Carolyn. Not only had she been fine when I was the one who got the necklace, but she was willing to attack with words and fists.

Angus now wore a huge white bandage over most of his head. He bit open a tiny white packet and held it up to his forehead. Take-away ketchup from a hamburger place. Fake blood. Finally Miranda and the others noticed him. "Who is that?" whispered Miranda.

Carolyn and I said nothing.

Miranda thought we should locate the parents in case the little boy was insane.

My soda can was perspiring against my ankle. I leaned down over my lap, and holding the can out of sight beneath my bleacher, I shook it vigorously.

"Ooooooh, look!" said Carolyn. "Brett's team is going to make a home run!"

This was mainly because nobody in the outfield was looking or could catch or, after they caught up to the ball, could throw. All the parents stood up and cheered madly for everybody and anybody.

"Miranda, you have a little brother or sister on one of these teams?" I asked.

"No, I just like to come."

"She just likes people around she can pick on," said Carolyn. "Everyone has a skill. That's Miranda's."

Miranda smiled proudly, her tiny teeth exposed like little beads.

She was watching Brett, though. I did not think it was teasing or nine-year-olds that brought Miranda to the games. I finished shaking my soda can.

"Has your mother admitted yet," Miranda asked Carolyn, "that Brett has moved out forever and doesn't even plan to finish high school? Has the chairman of the school board actually said out loud, 'Yes, my son is a high school dropout'?"

I held up my soda. "Want a sip, Miranda?" I aimed my can and yanked off the pull tab.

Soda sprayed two feet in the air. It dripped into Miranda's hair. It soaked into her T-shirt. It ran down her dangly earrings and hung like brown diamonds from her eyelashes. All the honeybees in Barrington deserted trash cans and flower beds to get better acquainted with Miranda.

"So, Carolyn," I said to her, over the sound of Miranda's screams, "when are you coming to visit us, anyway? I think you and I would get along—to use the perfect word—perfectly."

Chapter Nine

The family room off the kitchen had television, VCR, stereo, compact disc player, two computers, exercise bike, rowing machine, bookcases full of paperbacks, CDs, tapes and videos, and a fireplace with a raised hearth. Your old-fashioned people could start a fire and toast their toes or their marshmallows while your up-to-date people could check their e-mail, and your fitness people could slim down while your musicians could wear headphones. Wedged among this equipment were three enormous recliners, which, when tilted back with footrests up, missed the various components by an inch. Once positioned in a recliner, you stayed there, wrapped in a hand-crocheted afghan, while the person closest to the kitchen fed you.

Uncle Todd's recliner was dark and leathery, while Aunt Maggie's was ruffled and flowery. Carolyn, Annette and I fit on a double recliner, rather like an upholstered hospital bed that bent at the knees as well as the waist. Annette looked as nervous as somebody using a ski lift for the first time, perhaps expecting to be flattened inside the mechanism. The moment I tried out that recliner, I was addicted. It was the most comfortable, wonderful way to sit/lie/slouch. I felt decadent, a Roman aristocrat reclining for a feast. "All we need are the slaves," I told Carolyn.

"Angus?" she suggested. "How well trained is he?"

Annette and I laughed.

Angus of course was busy trying out headphones, synthesizers and the latest computer games, sorting through video selections and also starting a fire. Grandma said what with the air-conditioning and so forth, perhaps we didn't need that many logs, but Angus was safe inside his earphones and added every piece of kindling standing upright in a hammered-brass basket on the hearth. Grandma sat in a straight-backed kitchen chair. She can't slump now or it's permanent. "Aren't little boys wonderful?" she said of Angus.

Annette and I reserved comment.

Aunt Maggie said, "They are. I wish Brett would still—" She broke off. "What is everybody going to wear tomorrow night for the reunion party? Not that it matters, with Charlie not coming. I don't know how I'm going to face everybody.

I feel like the youngest kid in this room. All I want is to slug my big brother."

"Then this is a good time to tell Uncle Charlie stories," said Carolyn. She passed Annette an unappealing homemade snack—Cheerios, broken pretzels, peanuts and onion salt making a mess in the bowl—and Annette passed it along to me, and I passed it to Angus, who is an excellent garbage bag for food nobody else wants. I could hardly wait to hear all the wonderful Uncle Charlie stories.

"Uncle Charlie," said Carolyn happily, "is the black sheep of the family." She heaved herself out of our recliner and crawled over her father's extended feet, explaining that we needed a higher quality of snack down at our end of the room. "Everybody was always mad at Charlie," she said, heading for the kitchen, "and he was always having to run away or get divorced in order to escape."

Annette said she thought that was an oversimplification of the facts.

Uncle Todd said maybe he would tell Carolyn stories instead, like the time she sneaked into the state fair without buying a ticket on the same day the state police were trying to corner a gang of teenage pickpockets and—

"No!" yelled Carolyn, charging back into the room, armed with a half gallon of ice cream and a scoop. She had no bowls, and I hoped that we were just going to pass the ice cream around and lick. But she made a second trip for bowls and spoons.

"Your poor dad," Uncle Todd told me, "has become a Barrington myth. From what I see of Angus, there is a possibility of a second generation joining him."

"Was Daddy that bad?" I said nervously. I wasn't sure I wanted to hear any When Your Father Was a Boy stories after all.

"Your father was terrific," said Uncle Todd. "Speaking of course as a latecomer who missed the really good years. You're never bored around Charlie. Of course, people don't know the facts of situations like Toby, because along with everything else, Charlie keeps a great secret, and secrets generate gossip."

Angus was encased in his own noise. He did not hear the word Toby. Carolyn and Aunt Maggie did not look interested, and Annette was yawning. Grandma stood up slowly. "I believe I'm going to bed," she said, and Uncle Todd took her arm and escorted her to the guest room as if he were walking her down the aisle to seat her at a family wedding.

"Perhaps it's time for all of us to get some rest," said Aunt Maggie. "You three have had a hard day. All that travel. Of course I'm sure I won't sleep a wink, what with thinking about my ruined party."

Recliners popped back. Electronics were shut down and snacks collected.

I cannot bear to admit that I am ignorant. I don't care what it is—science class, new computer program, using a different subway—I can't stand to be the dumb one. It's as if I think I should have been born knowing everything. So if I said, "What are you guys talking about? Who is Toby?" I would feel as if the whole world were pointing and jeering. Uncle Todd thought my dad was terrific. All I had to say to my nice uncle was "So tell me about Toby. Because it's a secret from me, too."

But how could a hidden half brother be a good secret? How could it be anything but bad? And yet there didn't seem to be anything hidden about Toby. He was here, and they knew him, and Carolyn was friends with him, and Toby knew who I was, and had been invited to the party. If he's really my half brother, I thought, wouldn't I feel toward him what I feel toward Angus? Half yuck and half affection? Love that's just an affectionate state of being annoyed?

Ask, I told myself.

But I didn't.

Aunt Maggie showed Annette how to flatten one of the recliners completely and make it up for a bed. Annette did not look eager to sleep there.

We all drifted up to bed, except Angus, who wanted to stay up all night playing with electronic components. Annette would have said yes, since it was vacation and who cared anyway, and he could have had the recliner bed, and she would have slept in Brett's room on a mattress. But Aunt Maggie was the sort who believed that firm bedtimes created stable character, so Annette said, "Angus! Certainly not! It's bedtime!"

Angus looked as if he had not encountered this concept before, which all summer in Vermont he hadn't.

"And you have to get clean first," I said, because the shock of having to use soap would keep Angus from saying, "What do you mean—bedtime?"

"Oh, good!" said Angus, leaping up. "I get the bathroom first!"

Annette and I stared at him.

"The bathroom has a whirlpool," explained Angus. "You don't even need a washcloth in one of those. It just flicks the dirt off you, like a dishwasher."

Aunt Maggie followed Angus toward the bathroom.

"I don't need help!" he shrieked, horrified.

"I'm just going to show you how to turn everything on, and especially how to turn everything off," said Aunt Maggie. "Floods are so boring."

"Not to me," said Angus. But he was grinning at her, and she was half reassured that he wasn't intentionally going to flood the place just to get a little action going.

I picked up my necklace in its lovely case. "What present did Grandma give you, Carolyn?" I asked, and then was scared that maybe Grandma hadn't given Carolyn anything, and now I would have to offer to split the necklace or something.

Carolyn beamed. "Train tickets for the next time I visit her in Arizona. I don't want to fly. I want to take the train and look out the window at America."

We had never visited Grandma in Arizona. My mother was the one who had arranged family trips, and from the day she moved out to be with Jean-Paul, we hadn't had such a trip. Daddy couldn't put it together. It was Annette who put Vermont together.

Carolyn said, "How come Grandma didn't give you anything, Annette?"

"I'm too old for midsummer presents," said Annette. "Anyway, she's not my grandmother."

"True," said Carolyn. "And I suppose she's had so many daughters-in-law with Charlie that she can't be giving presents to every new bride every summer."

"Thank you for sharing that," said Annette.

We use them for our family joke, I thought. We say, "The Perfects wouldn't have a food fight now, would they?" They use us for their family joke. "How many wives is he up to now? Anybody kept count?"

It was fine for us to laugh at them, but it was not fine at all for them to laugh at us.

Aunt Maggie returned, wearing a satin bathrobe, lacy and fragile, like something in an old-fashioned trousseau. She held high on a padded velvet hanger a summery dress with tiny tucks and a flared skirt and tiny pottery planets on embroidered orbits facing a silver crescent moon.

"Oh, that's stunning!" cried Annette. "You will be the belle of tomorrow's ball."

"Somebody has to be something," said Aunt Maggie, "since the guest of honor isn't going to show up. What's your dress like?"

"Nothing compared to that," said Annette, touching the little solar system. Annette was a New Yorker. Even in summer, she was happiest wearing black. She had a crisp summer suit, with knee-length cuffed shorts and a soft white blouse with tuxedo pleats and a tiny black jacket with a black-and-white kerchief tucked in the tiny pocket and black-and-white beads to match black-and-white earrings. But since Annette could only choose clothing well, and not wear it well, she would look disheveled and hot.

She and Aunt Maggie would face the next day's party in outfits carefully chosen, leaving trails of perfume behind them, hoping nobody would know that they were cut to pieces inside. My father did indeed seem able to leave everybody in the lurch.

We slouched off to our rooms. I was tired from flight and family, but I wasn't sure I could ever fall asleep. "What's that over your bed?" I asked Carolyn. "Have you framed a baton?"

"It is a baton," she said, "and Brett framed it for me for a birthday present. When I was learning baton-twirling and hoping to make the team, Mom took a video. Of course, she takes hundreds of videos. I saw myself all worked up about my ability to catch a stick, and I realized that that's what I would be remembered for at my high school reunions. My ability to catch a stick. Brett thought it was hysterical and just right for my abilities as a human being. He began introducing me as his sister the dog. We'd be cleaning up the yard after a storm, and every twig and branch he'd pick up, he'd throw across the grass and yell, 'Fetch!' " Carolyn grinned at me. "So I quit twirling."

I have cried myself to sleep a few times in the past several years. It was much nicer to laugh myself to sleep.

In the morning Aunt Maggie strong-armed us onto chairs around the breakfast table. For a woman who does not believe in violence, she is very forceful. We had bacon, grapefruit halves, hot biscuits slathered with butter and honey, pan-fried potatoes, blueberry pancakes and tall glasses of orange juice. I don't usually have that much breakfast in a month.

Grandma told about how my father used to hold lawn-mowing races with his friends, and once, he got so excited, he mowed off the entire garden of the next-door neighbors. Aunt Maggie said that that very garden owner was coming to the surprise party that night with a little plaque commemorating the event, only of course Charlie, being Charlie, would not be there to receive it. Grandma told about how Daddy ran away from home three times when he was in junior high. "Didn't usually go very far," she said. "We found him once sleeping in the garage."

"Reminds me," said Uncle Todd. "Come on, Angus. You and I have chores to do in the garage."

"I hate chores."

"Me too. That's why I'm going to make you do all of them. Last one in the garage is a rotten egg," said Uncle Todd, taking a scoop of scrambled eggs in his bare hand. Angus was thrilled at the prospect of a food fight and let himself be chased into the garage.

"You know what I forgot to tell everybody?" I said. "Oh, gosh, I knew there was something important. I'm so sorry. I forgot to tell you Joanna's coming. She's flying in tomorrow. Isn't that fun? She'll be here too."

"That's wonderful!" cried Grandma. "I'm so happy. All five of my wonderful grandchildren will be together."

Aunt Maggie burst into tears.

"Now, Mom," said Carolyn, with the quick desperation I knew so well, the daughter thinking, I can smooth this over; I can make it all right; I can solve this. But she can't. "Brett has to come home eventually," said Carolyn. "Just because he wouldn't even talk to us at the baseball game doesn't mean he'll never live at home again. Johnny's parents will get sick of feeding Brett, and Brett's grown another inch and needs new clothes, and Johnny's parents surely won't buy somebody else's kid new jeans and sneakers. So Brett will have to come home."

"He won't have to!" said Aunt Maggie savagely. "He'll be just like his uncle Charlie and wander around town making friends with the scum of the earth and wearing sneakers he slices open to let his toes air out."

Angus had come back for another handful of scrambled egg. "Slicing out the toes of his sneakers?" he said eagerly.

"Get lost," I said to him, and he did, presumably because he had sneakers to deface.

The night before, after the Little League game, when Brett stood all dusty among his losing players, and his parents walked uncertainly toward him, I had seen in his face what Annette must have seen in mine and in Joanna's and in Angus's for a year and a half: a sneer and rejection.

You have so little power. You can't hold together your mother and father's marriage. You can't prevent them from remarrying strangers. You can't keep them from dividing up the furniture and the children and the calendar. But you can curl your lip, and make them wilt, and hurt them bad, and it's good. You're glad.

I hurt for Carolyn, though, the peacemaker. I hurt a little bit for Aunt Maggie, but not much, because she was doing exactly what Joanna had predicted she would do: saying bad things about our father.

"You must bring out the family photograph albums," said Annette. "I'd love to see Charlie like that."

"In all his teenage splendor," said Aunt Maggie grimly. It didn't sound as if she meant splendor; it sounded as if she meant dung-streaked horse blankets. "Brett thinks Charlie is somebody to *admire!*" Aunt Maggie burst out. "He thinks Charlie is somebody *special!* After all the hard work bringing my children up right, my own son turned out like *Charlie!*"

I opened my mouth to say a thing or two, but Annette shook her head very gently, and I let it go.

"I have to give this stupid party!" Aunt Maggie said, tossing dishes into the dishwasher like a woman who wants all-new china. Or a woman who would like to break her plates over her brother's head. "I had such fun planning this, and thinking about it, and getting every detail just right, and every single guest is going to know that my own son doesn't want to live with me and my own brother can't be bothered to show up." She slammed the door of the dishwasher and stormed out of the room.

There was silence.

Grandma stared into her coffee cup. Carolyn clung to her orange juice glass. Annette played with her sunglasses, horrid misshapen yellow things that are supposed to be fashionably retro but only make her look like a serial killer. I said, "We'll have to start calling Aunt Maggie Big Joanna. Absolutely identical temper tantrums."

Annette nodded. She could see the truth in that.

Carolyn wanted details, and my stepmother and I took turns telling about Joanna's temper, and then Grandma said, "Perhaps, darling, you should telephone Joanna and get the details of her plane flight. If indeed she hasn't left already.

Think of the temper tantrum she might have if she is sitting in the airport waiting to be picked up while we are sleeping in from the rigors of an unsuccessful surprise party."

It was ten A.M. in Barrington. It would be five P.M. in Paris.

My stepmother handed me her cell phone, and she and Carolyn and Grandma watched. I'd have to call Joanna right there, in front of everybody, and what if Mother or Jean-Paul answered? "I forget the number," I said.

"Your mother's phone number?" said Carolyn incredulously.

"Because she doesn't ever dial it, of course," said Annette, rescuing me. "It's in *her* phone's address memory," she lied, "but this is my phone. It's listed in my phone address book, Shelley."

Carolyn leaned forward eagerly to be part of the conversation.

"You'll want privacy, Shelley," Annette added. "Phone from Carolyn's bedroom."

Stepmother. It's not such a bad word after all, I thought. A mother, except a step below. I didn't want Annette to go back to work. I wanted her to stay with Angus and me, and be in Vermont, and forget Granger Elliott, and take us bagel-hunting in major cities.

I poked at Annette's phone. I could not believe that once in her entire acquaintance with Daddy she had ever even thought about calling my mother. I felt sure she would bungee jump without the cord before she would telephone my mother. But here was the number, neatly stored. For emergencies, I thought. Because in the end, Annette is not going to let me down. My real mother will let me down and go live across an ocean, and my real father will let me down, bailing out on important events, setting terrible examples and failing to support or acknowledge sons from previous marriages—but my stepmother will do the right thing.

This was so depressing I didn't care if I had to speak to Mother or Jean-Paul after all, and when it was Joanna who answered the phone, I wasn't even relieved. I was just irked that I had to deal with any of this. "Oh, hi, Jo," I said grumpily.

"Shelley!" cried my sister. "I was postponing calling you because I'm so upset. I'm so glad to hear your voice. I feel as if I've been here for a century. But I won't be coming after all, Shell. I'm staying here."

"Staying?" I whispered. "For good? You're never coming home?"

"No, no, no. I mean the reunion. Barrington. Mother started crying when I said I want to be with you guys. She hasn't stopped crying either. I hate it when parents have feelings. They should be like carvings. Solid. No emotions. And here's Mother sobbing all over the place because one month with her is plenty and I want my real family."

"Did you say that to her?" I asked. "Out loud? Real family?"

"Yes. I did it to hurt her, but I didn't think it would be so successful. Shelley, Mom needs me. I kicked her in the teeth and now—"

"You have to build her smile back," I said.

"If you would just talk to her once on the phone without sounding as if she's worse than anthrax, that would build up her smile."

"Me?"

"You're maddest of all of us."

"I am not."

"You are so. Tell me. When we finish talking, are you going to ask to speak to Mother?"

I said nothing.

"No, you're not. Because you're mad."

I said nothing.

"Mother says her three children have gone and grown up without her and she doesn't know us anymore and we'd all rather live somewhere else and we're still mad."

"What did she think would happen when she crossed the ocean?"

Joanna sighed. "Give everybody hugs for me. Have a great time for me." Her voice broke.

I couldn't even find my voice. "Bye," I whispered.

Chapter Ten

The party rental truck had arrived. Uncle Todd sent Angus into the kitchen to get volunteers to help distribute chairs and tables all over the yard and drape them with cushions and linens. There were no volunteers. Everybody was too busy listening to Aunt Maggie talk about loss and holes in families and pain between mothers and sons and the failure of brothers to have any value whatsoever on the face of the entire earth.

I was so mad.

I had just told Joanna that I didn't get mad, but now I was mad at Aunt Maggie and her dumb party and the entire town of Barrington and especially my father. You should be here! I yelled at him in my heart. You're making Annette and me defend you. You're ruining the party. You're not telling me who Toby is. And I have to listen to your sister whine about Brett, whose only problem is his father won't let him use the car.

I had a sudden memory of my mother, years ago, making pound cake. She had beaten the butter and sugar together with a wooden spoon instead of using her Cuisinart. "Does it taste better that way, Mommy?" I had asked, licking the bowl.

"No, but it feels better," said my mother. "Pounding a cake is usually more acceptable than pounding a person you're really mad at."

Oh, Mommy!

Who were you mad at? And how come I can't be little again, sitting on a stool so high that my feet swing in the air, wearing your old red-and-white-striped apron with the bib and licking the spoon from the cake you were baking?

Aunt Maggie noticed me. "When is Joanna's flight?" she said, in the voice of one asking when Joanna's kidney transplant was scheduled.

"She's not coming after all," I said. "I got overexcited. I misunderstood. She's staying in Paris."

Carolyn and Annette looked at me thoughtfully. Grandma said, "Oh, I'm so sorry she isn't coming. I miss her already."

Uncle Todd came in. "Come on, people. Help out here."

"Joanna isn't coming," said Aunt Maggie. "Brett isn't coming. Charlie isn't coming. Nobody's coming."

"We're coming," said Carolyn irritably. "Ninety-seven hungry people with packages to put on the gift table are coming. Shelley, let's do something interesting." We walked out the door into the backyard, where the only interesting possibility was unloading stacked plastic lawn chairs, so we walked around the other side of the house and into the front yard and stood beneath that blazing, stupefying Midwestern sun.

"How come they can't talk about me?" demanded Carolyn. "I'm here. I'm doing things right. But am I worth a conversation? Of course not."

"I know just how you feel," I said. "Let's go for a walk."

Carolyn stared at me. "I suppose we could," she said doubtfully, as if she had walked once a few years ago and maybe the skill would come back to her. City people walk so much more than town people, even in towns like Barrington, where everything is so close and there are lots of sidewalks.

"We'll be back later, Mom," shouted Carolyn toward the house, but of course nobody could hear; the windows were all closed to keep the air-conditioning in. We wandered down the block. Carolyn looked into yards and across intersections as if she were a tourist. "I haven't done this in ages," she confided.

We went block after block. We came to a stone church flanked by blooming shrubs and a glass-fronted announcement board for Sunday services. "Our church," said Carolyn. "We get to skip during the summer, but during the school year we go. Not Brett, of course. It would make my parents happy if he went, so it's the last thing he's going to do."

We didn't go to church except on Christmas and Easter, and I had never attended Sunday school. I was uneasy about admitting this. Carolyn might report to her mother, who probably ranked Sunday school even higher than backyards for creating stable families.

We walked on.

"There's Johnny Cameron's," said Carolyn.

The Cameron house was being relandscaped. Brand-new shrubs, the size of footballs, stood at attention in straight lines. Tiny trees, tethered by wires thicker than their branches, were placed at regular intervals. Sprinklers in a newly installed underground system tried unsuccessfully to keep the grass seeds damp under the hot sun.

I wondered what kind of people Mr. and Mrs. Cameron were, and whether Brett was happy living with them, and whether they would in fact buy him new sneakers. I said, "Where does Toby live?"

"Chicago, of course," said Carolyn. "He's staying with his grandparents, though. Celeste's parents. They never approved of Charlie."

"Will they be at the party?" I asked.

"No. But Toby will. He's always wanted to meet Charlie, of course. And now he won't. But who cares about any of them? I care about me. You know the parable of the prodigal son?"

I didn't know the words *parable* or *prodigal*, so I just said, "Not really."

"It's a story Jesus tells. There are these two sons, see. The bad one leaves home. He parties, he takes drugs, he hangs out with scum. The parents never hear from him. The good one stays home and does all the chores for his father and runs the farm. One day the bad kid comes back and says he's sorry. The father is so happy, he throws a big party. But all the time the good kid was being good, the father never once even thought of throwing a party for him."

Carolyn walked like a person eager to kick a dog. "I bet anything," she said, "that I'll stay home being good year in and year out, and the most they'll ever give me is new spiral-bound notebooks every September. But the minute Brett comes back in the door, it'll be a new car, a new computer and a winter vacation on a Florida beach."

We detoured into the street to avoid being soaked by lawn sprinklers, and then the water looked pretty good, so we walked through it and cooled off.

"I am completely sick of being a nice person," said my cousin. "I feel like puncturing a few tires."

"You know, you're not bad, Carolyn. Can I stay here all summer?"

"No. It's my turn to go somewhere. I get to go back to Vermont with you."

"That would be great. I'll tell Annette. She's pretty relaxed about stuff, really. She has low expectations after a year and a half of Angus."

We walked on in companionable sweatiness.

A car straight off one of the posters that Joanna and I paper our apartment bedroom with pulled up next to us: a 1963 maroon Cadillac convertible. It was packed with girls our age, twice as many girls as space or seat belts, and driven by a hugely overweight man. "Carolyn!" they yelled. "You forgot Pammy's birthday party!"

"Hi, Pammy!" shrieked Carolyn. "I didn't forget! I RSVP'ed that I couldn't come because I was setting everything aside for my cousins."

We hadn't set aside anything when Brett and Carolyn visited us in New York. We never even thought of setting anything aside.

"We tracked you down, though," said the fat man. "What's a party without a Preffyn? Come on, you two, get in! And you must be Charlie's girl Shelley. Glad to meet you, Shelley."

Carolyn clambered right over the side of the Caddy and fell messily into the laps of the other girls. "Come on, Shell," she said over her shoulder.

The girls wedged into the beautiful convertible seemed younger and gigglier than I was. Carolyn blended in. She ceased to be my cousin. I couldn't tell her apart from the others. I was afraid of them all, suddenly, as if they were not a bunch of laughing girls on their way to a birthday party, but a pack of wild dogs.

"No, you go on," I said quickly. "I'll walk on home and make sure Annette's okay. Help Aunt Maggie get set up and stuff."

"I'll get you guys back home in time," the driver assured me. "You won't be late to Charlie's party. I'm coming myself. Went to school with your dad, you know. Yup. Graduated the year after him."

"Oh, Mr. Hallahan," said Carolyn, beating on his shoulder as if he were her property. She must have known him, and his daughter Pammy, if I was adding this up right, for a long time. "My mother didn't remember to tell the guest of honor to come on the right date. Charlie won't be here."

Mr. Hallahan laughed hugely. "That's our boy Charlie," he said.

I thought it was actually our girl Maggie, but I was polite and begged Carolyn to attend the birthday party without me, and off they went. I stood alone in Barrington. I felt misplaced. I walked slowly back the way we'd come, pausing at each corner as if I thought something might go wrong.

And something did.

* * *

How dumb daydreams can be.

I found myself facing the Camerons' house. I had not even managed to say hello to my cousin Brett the night before, he had kept such a distance. I went up and knocked on the front door. After all, these must be pleasant people, the sort of loving, generous folk who took in kids in trouble. They would answer the bell exclaiming, "Charlie's daughter!" Brett would say, "Gosh, I'm glad you came. I really need a cousin to escort me home so I can apologize and get along with my mother again."

That was my daydream.

And I, the essential follower—the one who tags after Bev or Kelsey or Marley in the city, and after Angus in Vermont, and after Carolyn that day—I led the way. I went alone up to a stranger's house to interfere with somebody's life.

"Oh, hi," said Brett without interest. "It's you."

Brett seemed so much older than I had expected. His tan was not golden like his sister's or Toby's, but dark and hard. He wore reflective sunglasses that hid a third of his face, even though he was indoors. I didn't feel related to him at all. Where was the cousin I had played with in distant summers? The cousin who had lowered his bike seat for me so I could ride more easily? The cousin who had found Band-Aids when I scraped my knee? The cousin who had given me his ice cream cone when I played too hard and the ice cream fell out of my cone and onto the sidewalk?

The front door opened directly into the living room. Behind Brett, a tall, thin boy stared at me. Brett did not introduce me. Motionless on the couch was Miranda. The three of them were watching television. There were no adults around. The house had a thick smell, as if garbage needed to be emptied and sheets needed changing. The acrid scent of cigarettes was strong. The shades had been pulled down, and the rooms were dim and sullen. Who would run away from Aunt Maggie's sparkling home to this?

Somebody either desperate or stupid.

"Whaddaya want?" said Brett.

"Just to say hello." I was flustered. "We haven't had a chance to see each other yet."

"Oh, wow, Brett, what an honor," said Miranda. "The cousin from New York City going out of her way for a little down-home chat."

The thin boy laughed. Miranda laughed. Brett remained behind his silver lenses.

"Are you coming to the party tonight?" I said, knowing how pathetic I sounded.

"Why would I want to hang out with that bunch of assholes?" said Brett.

The word shocked me. Not because I hadn't heard it before, but because it meant us: Uncle Todd, Aunt Maggie, Grandma, Annette, me, Carolyn, Angus. The word was so ugly, so mean.

"Your own father couldn't be bothered to come," said

Brett. "What makes you think I'd make any more effort than he does?"

No reason came to mind.

"Aren't you supposed to be helping with the big event?" he said. "The big failure, I should say. Since as usual our sainted mother figured she could engineer everybody else's lives without asking first."

Poor Aunt Maggie. They were so mad at her. But we had been mad at her too, since the divorce. Aunt Maggie went on relentlessly, cheerfully, faultlessly, no matter what was going on around her. Aunt Maggie was Perfect.

Miranda flicked the remote control at high speed. Scraps of dialogue, bits of advertisements, two notes of a theme song and a burst of applause were tossed into the room like broken lives. I was afraid of these three. This was what giving up looked like. Shuttered and dusty and mean-mouthed. I would rather be like Aunt Maggie any day.

I backed toward the door.

"Have a nice day," said Miranda.

I stumbled out, shutting the door behind me, and ran down the street, thankful for every house and tree and fence that protected me from them.

Nobody ever solved a problem by shutting out the air and the family. Except me. I had shut out my mother. Shut out her entire world. Hid from her. Just like Brett.

I stopped running. The Barrington sun was frying me like

an egg. My hair turned sticky. Even my thoughts stuck together.

How could I be the one who was wrong? Other people were the wrongdoers; I got dragged along. I made none of those awful decisions, filed none of those awful divorce papers.

I found myself not on Carolyn's road, but a block over from the little stone church, on the quiet, half-occupied old main street. Parallel parking was neatly marked in front of its old-fashioned stores, and most slots were empty. When I was little, my mother had taken us to a drugstore on this street, and we had gotten something called a root beer float. But nobody anymore would have a soda fountain in a drugstore.

I walked past each store, little places that probably couldn't afford rent at a mall. Sewing machine repair, silk flowers, Thai takeout, secondhand paperbacks, children's dance school, real estate agent.

And a drugstore. And inside it, an ice cream parlor.

It wasn't exactly what I remembered, but then, neither was Brett. At least this was sunny and bright with little glass tables and little round-bottomed chairs and zinnia bouquets on each table. The zinnias sold me. I fished in my jeans pocket to see how much money I had.

The ice cream choices were written on a blackboard in colored chalk. I could have pumpkin-pie ice cream or pink peppermint or mocha cream peanut butter. Somebody else came into the ice cream parlor and stood right behind me, then shifted next to me. I half looked. Old jeans into whose pockets were jammed big masculine hands. Old T-shirt. Big elbows.

I'll have chocolate, I thought, the way I always do.

I looked a little more closely at the person in the old T-shirt and the old jeans.

It was Toby.

Chapter Eleven

Here's why I don't like to ask questions.

It's not because I'm afraid of the answers.

I just don't think there should be any questions to start with. Your father should be your father; he should be married to your mother; you should all live happily ever after. And that's that.

"Hi, Shelley," said Toby eagerly.

He was as handsome as he had been the afternoon before. "Let's share a table," he said. "Come on." He nudged me forward. The waitress followed us, envious of me. I ordered a chocolate sundae, and he ordered butterscotch on vanilla. We were obviously not the kind to experiment with important things like ice cream. Toby got straight to the point. Looking anxious, because it mattered, he said, "Does your father ever talk about me?" He dipped his spoon into his sundae and had an enormous butterscotch-dripping mouthful of vanilla.

I could not really breathe.

Breathing is essential to speech. I clung to my small paper napkin and ran out of air.

"I've always wanted to meet Charlie," said Toby, looking up from his ice cream and into my eyes. What was he looking there for? Blood ties? You wouldn't think, under the circumstances, that his attention could be so evenly divided between the topic of discussion and the ice cream.

"I owe him a lot," Toby added.

I wanted to run. Like Angus. The whole way home, to Vermont or New York City. I understood Angus, slamming a door, hiding out.

Families and divorce and secrets are like history-class discussions of World War III or nuclear bombs. Everybody gets extremely intense for forty-five minutes and says profound things and considers the doom of mankind. But then the bell rings, and you have important things to consider, like whether to lend your best friend those silver-and-turquoise earrings, whether to go to the game with your buddies or to the library and start the research paper due tomorrow, which you should have started a month ago.

A month ago Angus had handed me a bomb, and when I thought about it, I was afraid and sweaty and angry. But mostly I didn't think about it. You can't think about a bomb any more than you can think about your own parents' divorce until it's there and it's in your lap, which is filling with tears.

I could use a bomb shelter right now, I thought. Because I think old Toby here is about to drop a bomb. "You owe him a lot?" I repeated, trying to be calm and ordinary. I paid close attention to how I held my spoon. I kept control over the corners of my mouth, which were trying to tremble.

Like, what was owed? Life? Breath? Genes?

Joanna and I had giggled and teased on the phone when we considered a hidden half brother. She was rather thrilled by it. But it was not thrilling. It was sick and terrible.

Can I still love Daddy if he's really bad? I thought. If he couldn't be a father to Toby at all, then is he a good father? Even to me?

"If your father hadn't paid the bills," said Toby, "I don't know where we'd be now. I mean . . ."

Toby said "I mean" as if it were a whole sentence, as if nobody, including Toby, could possibly know what he meant.

"You read about terrible divorces and horrible betrayals," said Toby, "or if you like talk shows, the kind where they do relationships, you listen to people who hate the person they once loved, and they trick them and spit on them."

No. I didn't read about them. I didn't listen to them. I didn't watch them. Who needed reading material when she could just live through it?

"And your father," said Toby.

Toby's technique of using short little phrases as if they were long, detailed explanations was giving me a headache.

"Well, he's your father," said Toby. "But he paid for me."

"Paid for you?" I echoed stupidly.

Toby looked at me oddly. And then he seemed as upset as I was. "You don't know anything?"

"He's never even mentioned you," I said. "I don't know a single thing."

Toby stared down into his ice cream. He gave a funny little laugh. "I don't know whether to feel rotten about that or not."

"I feel rotten," I said. My tears dropped with surprising weight, not blending into my ice cream, but lying in tiny tear puddles on top.

"Don't cry," whispered Toby, appalled. "It's not your fault."

"But it's terrible! He should have told us about you."

"It's not that terrible," protested Toby.

"Not to tell us that he has another son?"

Toby's jaw grew slack. Then he rolled his eyes. "Carolyn and Brett been getting back at you for all the times you conned them in New York? Shelley, your father isn't my father. I'm not your brother. The only son he has is Angus. Which, from what I've heard about Angus, is a good thing."

"You're not my brother?"

"How could I be your brother?"

"Angus said Daddy had a son named Toby."

"Oh. Angus probably overheard something and got it wrong, like half this dumb, gossipy town. My mother and your father hardly even got married before they separated. They were only sixteen, remember. Back then you had to quit high school if you were married, and so they couldn't go to school, and they weren't earning any money, and the dishes got dirty, and the car ran out of gas, and my mother went to live with her aunt in Chicago, and your father hitch-hiked to New York. And they each went back to school and finished college, and the funny thing was, they stayed in love, even though they couldn't stand living together, or dealing with Barrington gossip and relatives. I mean, Shelley, you just can't imagine gossip in a small town. Me from Chicago and you from New York—we don't know gossip, not the way our parents do." He drank some Coke. "Celeste and Charlie were the focus of the town's attention, because she was the girl everybody had expected to go out and be a stunning female success, and your father was the boy who should have founded a major corporation or be-come president."

For a moment I could see them: my father, golden and

133

blurred—only two years older than I am now—overcome by Celeste's lovesick eyes; two kids running away to find perfection and landing in pain. "Don't stop," I ordered Toby. "Tell me the rest."

"You never heard any of this?" He was amazed and definitely hurt.

"Daddy never talks about Celeste. We only know about her from family gossip."

Toby nodded, but it was the kind of nod of somebody who doesn't understand. He wanted Daddy to have talked about it, I thought. Toby was sure he was special enough for my father to share him with us.

I stirred my tears into the ice cream and wondered if it would taste different.

Perhaps there is no time when a secret is a good thing. Perhaps for every person you protect, you damage another one. But who could know that? Who could weigh whether protection or exposure matters more?

"They used to telephone each other whenever one of them had enough money for the long-distance phone bill," said Toby, half laughing, abbreviating a beloved story he had heard a hundred times. "Your father and my mother. They just didn't know what to do. My mother says they were afraid to meet each other again. On the phone, they could be kind and affectionate, because she was in Chicago and he was in New York. They were afraid that if they both went to

Barrington, or visited each other, or met in the middle, they'd fight again."

I tried to imagine them, hundreds of miles of phone line between them, separate apartments and lives, but I couldn't do it this time; the images didn't appear. I could see Daddy only as the man I knew, a bear who laughed at everything and charged right on.

"I guess they were really just kids," said Toby dubiously.

I crossed Daddy and Angus in my mind. If I made Angus taller and older, locked into marriage, which was surely a lot scarier than a backyard bomb shelter, I could half see Daddy. I knew he'd put himself through NYU going nights. I knew that by the time I was born, he was already a success. But I had not known he saved money for a phone call to the high school sweetheart who wore his ring but lived in another state. If e-mail had existed back then, they could have talked for free. Maybe they would have settled their differences, communicating all day and all night.

"But then they each fell in love again," said Toby. "Your father fell in love with your mother, and my mother fell in love with my father. By then they'd been apart for years. Their divorce made them sad. I think they felt that instead of marrying other people, they should have remarried each other and tried again. But they didn't."

"Just as well. We wouldn't exist."

Toby finished his sundae and looked longingly at the

bottom of the dish, as if hoping it would spontaneously re-generate a second helping. "Anyway, when I was very little, my father got killed in a car accident, just after he had sunk every cent into a new business. There was nothing left. Not a dollar. And instead of turning to relatives in Barrington, who would know all, tell all and remember all for genera-tions, my mother asked your father for money. She thought he would lend her a little to keep her and me going until she could figure out what to do next."

I was starting to cry again. "And did he?"

"I can't believe you don't know any of this."

"Believe it. And tell me everything."

"He supported us the whole time my mother was in law school. Three years. Mom says if it hadn't been for Charlie, she would have been in some office pool, entering data or processing checks or something. We'd be on food stamps in-stead of skiing in Europe."

I knew that all my life I would remember this table in this drugstore. The way Toby folded his napkin into a dinosaur. The way his hands looked—large, nervous hands, playing with paper and spoons to keep occupied. The way my hands looked—rigid, because I was afraid that instead of playing with spoons I would grab Toby's hands and hold them per-manently.

"You going to finish your ice cream or not?" Toby said. Boys can always concentrate on the important things, like food.

"Not."

"How come?"

"I'm too nervous to swallow."

Toby thought about this. Nothing, including the final bomb and the end of humanity, would stop a boy from eating.

"You eat it," I said.

"You sure?"

"I'm sure. Just keep talking."

He was obedient. Aunt Maggie would not have approved of his table manners. He drank, spooned and talked at the same time. It was a very chocolatey recital. "Your father, Shelley, sent money for no reason except that they had loved each other once. He wrote that if they'd had a kid, he would have loved that kid, and he would love any child of hers, and he was glad to help. Mom still has the letter."

Toby, the child my father had loved, sat across from me, having my ice cream. I said, "Toby, I can't help it. I'm going to cry. A whole lot."

Toby looked alarmed. "In here? Noisily? Attracting attention?"

"Or we could go outside."

"You can't stop yourself?"

"I don't have a Delete Emotion button."

"Sure you do. Everybody does. Come on. There's a dinky little traveling fair around the corner. I'll take you on the roller coaster."

"I hate roller coasters. If you think it's bad when I'm trying not to cry, meet me when I'm trying not to throw up."

"Nah, this is really dinky, for three-year-olds and their five-year-old big brothers." Toby put money on the table to pay for both of us and stood up and took my hand. It was where my hand had wanted to be for a while now.

Toby said, "Barrington somehow found out that your father was sending Celeste child support. They figured it meant I'm his kid, which I am not. You are. Angus is. What's her name is. But my father was named Richard Donnelly, and I look like him and everything." Toby grinned, throwing in a little visual proof. Then he tightened his grip on my hand, partly because we were crossing the street and he seemed unsure that I possessed this skill, and partly because it was punctuation for his sentences. "My mother says there isn't much in Barrington but corn, relatives and rumors. So of course for the big reunion party, all of Barrington is talking, because I'm visiting my grandparents, who were once your father's in-laws, and I'm invited to the party, and they're not. But that's because my mother, Celeste, felt that it was asking an awful lot of Charlie to face every single person he knew in high school, and all his relatives, and her son, and the ex-in-laws. Plus she figured your stepmother, who she says is a lucky woman to be married to Charlie, deserved some kind of break."

Outside, summer was as strong as a hurricane. In New York summer means gasping for breath and hoping there will be no blackout to knock out the air-conditioning. In Vermont summer means the lake, and the deep green forest, and quiet. But in Barrington summer is a living thing, the burnished brilliance of sun and sky, a heat so great it lives on you and in you, ruling your body and your thoughts. I wanted to embrace summer if I could not embrace Toby. The heat was enough to bake away care, and broil off worry.

"I've always wanted to meet Charlie," said Toby. "When my mother talks about him, it's not the way anybody else talks about an ex-husband. She still loves him. Not getting-married type love. Not in-love type love. But . . . well . . . love."

And here I had thought I wasn't going to cry. I cried. Tears trailed down my face, and I had to tilt my head back to keep my contacts in place. The wind lifted my hair off my neck and threw grit on my tear tracks. "How old are you, anyway?"

"Sixteen. That's another thing. When your father started supporting us, he already had one little kid of his own, and then you were born and he had two little kids of his own, and still he was supporting us. You and your sister. What's her name?"

Nobody refers to Joanna as "what's her name." "Joanna," I said. "I think Daddy's always had extra money, though."

"Listen. People can have ten million extra dollars and still not share one dime with their ex-wife."

Toby bought us entrance tickets. Fifty cents. It really was a dinky little fair. It had only six rides. I opted for a small children's ride. Toby paid a quarter for each of us, and we climbed on merry-go-round horses. An aqua horse with a white mane for me, and red with a black mane for Toby. We were the only people riding. The music wound itself up, and slowly the horses began to circle. When Toby was up, I was down. We waved at each other, and our knees bumped.

"Where is your father that he can't make it to the party?" asked Toby.

"Oh, he's working for this big company that just got a new chairman of the board and a new CFO, and of all things, this weekend they're having a bonding retreat in the wilderness and he can't miss it." How odd that my father needed to go anywhere to bond with anybody. Charlie was the bond-master. Nobody bonded as well as Charlie. He must be teaching the seminar.

We rode the merry-go-round seven times, walking among the horses as it circled and making sure that we rode on every horse. Then we even rode the two ducks that didn't go up and down and were meant for moms with babies in their laps.

All along, I had never minded the Perfects or anybody else being Perfect as long as we had some Perfection too. I had a better father than anybody. A father who was always there, and funny, and strong, and who gave us bear hugs and took us to the lake or the movies and loved doing it.

Okay, I thought, so he has divorces and he skips out on surprise parties. He's still Perfect. He never stopped being Perfect.

The booths held green teddy bears you could win by throwing darts or shooting air guns or tossing beanbags. They sold fried dough and cotton candy, foot-long hot dogs, corn dogs and soft ice cream. They sold T-shirts with monster faces, and tacky jewelry with misspelled names.

We did every booth. "I hope we don't win anything," I told Toby. "I don't know what I would do with a mirror that has a beer ad printed on it."

When I looked at my watch, it was five o'clock in the afternoon. "Oh, no! Toby! I'm going to miss the party too! Everybody but me is already there!"

I bet Aunt Maggie doesn't know about Daddy supporting Toby, I thought suddenly. How could she say the things she says about him if she knew this? She'd want Brett to be exactly like Daddy if she knew.

Why did Daddy keep it such a secret?

We left the little fairground and walked back. There were sidewalks all the way. Toby did not take my hand. He talked about all kinds of stuff, and I hardly heard any of it because I was involved in an inner debate about whether I should take *his* hand.

The views in Barrington were longer than in Vermont. Trees in Vermont stalk the hillsides and meadows like vandals, filling every space. Beyond the edges of Barrington, the horizon swooped under blue armloads of sky, stretching to unknown farms and fields, and even to distant states and prairies. Hay had been cut. It was bleaching in the sun. It smelled wonderful and safe.

"Do you think Brett will come home?" I interrupted.

Toby didn't mind the interruption. "Sure. Eventually. Brett is kind of ordinary, you know. It's tough being ordinary when your parents want you to be incredibly special."

We were the only people using the sidewalk. City people walk everywhere. Country people use cars. "I'm ordinary," I pointed out.

"*You?*" Toby stared at me.

We crossed the final street. A block away you could tell that Aunt Maggie and Uncle Todd were having a huge party. Cars lined the road and were parked on lawns and doubled up in driveways. Balloon bouquets were tethered to the mailbox and fence and lamppost. The rich scent of meat cooking on hot coals permeated the neighborhood. The sound of the band throbbed generously.

"I've always sort of thought of you guys as relatives," said Toby shyly, "even though you aren't. Do you mind?"

I had not been thinking of Toby as a cousin. "As long as you promise not to be my brother," I said, "you can be any relative you want."

Toby's grin was nothing like my father's. Nothing like Angus's or DeWitt's or Uncle Todd's; it was his, and I quivered and I wanted that grin to be mine. I wanted to make that grin surface just for me, and I wanted it to vanish when I needed Toby to be serious.

I looked away from him. A couple was getting out of their car, the husband carrying a platter of brownies, and the wife balancing a lemon meringue pie. I love how in Barrington, even if you have your party catered, people will always contribute food, and it will be reliable food that you've seen before and you know well.

"I really wish Daddy could be here after all," I babbled. "Look at all the food. And all the friends. Are you staying long enough in Barrington to meet Daddy when he comes late? Annette thinks he'll be here on Wednesday. I don't think we have the actual flight time or anything, but as soon as we hear from him, I can tell him you're waiting."

A woman with a glass bowl of fresh strawberries and a can of Reddi-Wip crossed the grass and disappeared into the backyard, where the party was. Out of the back of their car, the next couple maneuvered a huge sheet cake and a sign that read

!!!!!!!!WELCOME HOME CHARLIE!!!!!!!!

Angus would love that cake. He's crazy about icing. He always scrapes away the best flowers and ribbons on the icing and leaves the insides for me.

"See you around," said Toby.

"Aren't you coming?"

"Nah."

"But I thought—I mean, you were invited. Please come."

Toby shook his head. I could not read his smile. It seemed uncertain, as if all the fears that he had taken away from me, he had been forced to keep for himself.

He turned his head aside. In profile he was bony and thin. When he turned back, the thinness went away, and he was handsome and nervous. It was like looking at two different people. I wanted to get to know him. To find out whether his profile or his full face represented the real Toby, or whether, as with so many people, his features had nothing at all to do with his personality.

I did not want to join the party. I stood looking at him, and he at me, and whether he was thinking of fathers, I do not know, but I was drowning in a hundred thoughts that had nothing to do with parents. Thoughts that prickled through my skin and flushed my cheeks.

Toby said, "Maybe tomorrow, Shelley? We could talk more. I could borrow my grandmother's car. We could go somewhere."

I nodded. "I'd like that."

Toby gave me a light kiss on the forehead and walked away.

Chapter Twelve

"Where have you been?" demanded Carolyn. "My mother is furious. Your family does disappearing jobs like nobody on earth." She bundled me up to her bedroom to get properly dressed. I was dusty and tear-streaked, so I hopped in the shower while she shouted through the crack in the bathroom door. "What are you going to wear, Shelley? This little white dress? With the pretty little embroidered roses?"

"I don't want to wear that after all. It's stupid. I'll be embarrassed."

"I have a nice pair of paisley shorts you could borrow."

"I hate paisley. It looks like pregnant worms." I came out of the shower. Carolyn combed my wet hair and said it wasn't fair for some people to have great hair like mine when people like her had to put up with crummy old ordinary hair.

I had always thought my hair was crummy old ordinary hair.

Carolyn snorted. Then she pulled another outfit from her closet. "How about my yellow two-piece dress? With the bare midriff."

I looked down at my bare midriff.

"I have little yellow sandals to go with it," coaxed Carolyn.

"Earrings?"

She handed me earrings. Little dangly yellow airplanes, which I would never have bought or put on my earlobes. But I gathered my courage and wore all of it, and I especially loved the part of my body where I had no clothing: my bare midriff.

Carolyn was wearing a bright red shirt, bright blue shorts, a bright purple belt and a bright green scarf. She looked like a crayon box. I wasn't sure I approved of that much color all at the same time.

Carolyn braided three very narrow cornrows to keep my hair away from the right side of my face and let the earring show, and then she used a hot curler to make a banana curl on the other side for contrast. "I bet you and Joanna fix each other's hair all the time, huh?" she said longingly.

"No, mostly we just fix Joanna's hair."

"That rots," said Carolyn. "What good is a sister if you're just her servant?"

We talked about sisters and brothers and whether we had any use for them. "Guess what," she confided. "Brett's coming home."

"That's wonderful. How did it happen?"

"Mom and Dad went over to the house where he's staying and confronted the parents. Mr. and Mrs. Cameron agreed that by giving Brett a free room and free food, they were aiding and abetting his running away. Like accessories to the crime. So they gave Brett an ultimatum. He can't stay at their house another night." Carolyn was both delighted and angry. "He'll get his welcome-home party," she said. "He'll slip into the backyard after dark tonight and help himself to somebody's apple pie, and Grandma will give him ten hundred hugs, and we'll all pretend nothing happened."

How different from my family. Of course, we can't pretend. Mommy did cross the ocean to live with Jean-Paul. Daddy is married to Annette.

Mommy, I thought. I'm calling her Mommy again.

Something in me had softened. Joanna had been right. I was the one who was maddest of all. And I never even knew it.

I said, "But how do you know Brett will come home? What if he just finds another friend to live with? Or hitch-hikes away?"

Carolyn gasped. It had not occurred to her that there could be anything other than a happy ending. An easy ending.

"I'm mad at Brett," she said, "but I want things to be the same. I want him to come home. Now."

I was about to tell her that things are never the same, and coming home doesn't change things back to where they were. Instead, I said, "Toby took me to the kiddie fair."

"*Toby?*" Carolyn did not let me down. "Oh, Shelley! Toby is so cute. Isn't he the cutest person in this state? I've wanted Toby to take me someplace ever since I can remember. Now, tell the truth. Did he take you to discuss family secrets or to take you?"

"I don't know the truth about that," I said.

"You have to tell me when you do know, or I'll make your life miserable," said Carolyn.

"Tell me that story again," I said. "The progidal one."

"Prodigal," she corrected.

"What's that mean? Do you have a dictionary?"

"It means wasteful," said Carolyn, who explained that she had done more than her fair share of Sunday school, she had probably done my share as well, and frankly she wanted me to take up the slack now.

"Wasteful?" I repeated, remembering the story. "Of what?"

"His inheritance. His family's love and patience. Because he ran off and was bad and did drugs and slept around and gambled and all that."

"Did they do drugs in biblical days?"

"No, but you're supposed to update everything. Like instead of leprosy, now you say AIDS. Listen," said Carolyn, "I don't want to be a Sunday school teacher. Let's go party."

So who was prodigal? I asked myself. Was I the one being wasteful of my family's love and patience? Was I ready now to come home to Mommy? Or was Mommy the one being wasteful of my love and patience, and now I was letting her come home to me?

We went downstairs. I loved my yellow dress. I felt older and prettier and barer. Especially my hair felt great. Carolyn was excellent with hair.

"It doesn't seem to be set up like a surprise party," I said, waving at the cars parked for blocks and the people dancing in the backyard and the side yard, on the driveway and over the grass.

"Once everybody found out that the Major Character was skipping," explained Carolyn, "they said they were coming when they felt like it instead of hiding out until the signal was given. So they're all here hours early, and my mother is a wreck."

"She should rejoice because her party is going to be such a success even without Daddy."

"Not my mother. She likes things to follow her master plan."

I was only fourteen, and nobody had followed my master plan yet.

The back steps led down to a deck, where groups of people stood among long tables of food the caterer had brought, while way out beyond the pool, Uncle Todd supervised a huge grill, where he was cooking hamburgers and hot dogs and barbecued ribs. I threaded my way among huge open coolers filled with ice and drinks in cans.

Carolyn darted off into the grass to greet somebody who immediately shouted about how tall she had gotten. The most boring thing about reunions is that everybody has to comment on how tall you have gotten.

I found a little step at the utility room door where I could stand high and survey the territory.

Angus was circulating. He had a notebook with him and was attacking each guest with pencil poised. I didn't cringe. I didn't want to abandon the party, and I didn't want to break his pencil or his head in half. It was Angus's project, not mine. For the very first time in my life as older sister, I didn't panic that people would point to me and say, "She's related to him. She's probably weird too."

I had been living through Angus for months. Maybe since Mommy left. I had been letting Angus do everything that took daring. I had been laughing at Angus's antics instead of coming up with my own. I had thought about Angus so I wouldn't have to think about me. Angus was my movie rental; I played him over and over instead of making my own film.

Time to make my film, I thought. Angus can direct his movie; I'll direct mine.

I would be beautiful and always wear my hair dramatically, like this, with each side different, and wild earrings that accentuated my long neck. Toby would be in the film, of course, and I'd have fast cars and dancing. Angus would not have a part. He was just a little boy. I was going to be a young woman wearing my grandmother's engagement necklace to formal events.

I walked off the deck and into the yard and approached a pair of total strangers and introduced myself. Lifetime first.

They were delighted to meet me. They were great fans of Charlie. "Is that your brother over there?" said the man, laughing. "He's the kid with the toilet paper at the ball game, huh? I laughed so hard. He's been collecting autographs all over town today. Is he Charlie Wollcott's kid or what? Walks up to complete strangers: 'Can I have your autograph?' and they say, 'But I'm nobody,' and the kid says, 'It's for my father. You aren't nobody to him. He'll want everybody's autograph since he can't be here himself.' Bet the kid's got a couple hundred autographs in that notebook so far to give to Charlie."

"That's adorable," said the wife.

"Charlie probably pays the kid to be different," said the husband.

I circulated.

I even considered modeling myself after Aunt Maggie, who was definitely the queen of circulating at parties. She laughed and kissed and laughed and waved and laughed and chattered.

If you're a late bloomer like me, you think a lot about age and whether people match their own ages. Aunt Maggie was a middle-aged body with a high school girl inside. You would not be surprised if she started talking about classes and boys and whether she really did eat nutritious stuff from the cafeteria or just had potato chips. Is that why she's on the school board? I wondered. To stay a teenager?

The menu was basically everything. If the catering people had brought it, it was beautifully presented. But most people hung out where Uncle Todd was: at the grill.

The dessert table was removed from the rest of the food. It was about ten feet long with a double row of cakes and pastries and tarts—anything you ever needed with butter, eggs and cream.

"Do I have to eat any real food," asked Angus, "or can I go straight to desserts?"

Angus was being passed from guest to guest like an appetizer so they could all exclaim, "Oh, this has to be Charlie's son!"

They knew I was Charlie's daughter and Annette was Charlie's wife, but the two of us together weren't half as exciting as Charlie's son.

I couldn't decide what to eat. There were too many choices. I stood in the corner of the yard where the edge of the yellow awning was brushed by the lowest branch of the great maple tree. In the lowering sun I was just another gold-edged shadow.

A teasing voice said, "Now, how many wives is it so far? What number is Charlie up to? Five? Six?"

Aunt Maggie giggled, sounding like Joanna. "Shhh," said my aunt. "The children are very defensive. Don't let them hear you."

Somebody came up behind me. Toby, I thought. He changed his mind.

But it was Annette and Angus. "Has anybody on earth really had five or six wives?" muttered Angus.

"Henry the Eighth of England," said Annette. "He was always getting married again. Sometimes he divorced the old one, but mostly he just cut off her head."

Angus was awestruck. "Why would anybody marry him after that? I bet the girls were nervous about marrying a guy that cut off three or four heads in a row."

Annette said that was one of the mysteries of history.

Angus thought he would bail on the party, take his dessert selections inside and go look up Henry the Eighth on the Internet. Then he changed his mind. He would start a new autograph collection. He would ask every man at this party exactly how many wives *he* had had and see whether or not our father came in with the highest score.

Annette said perhaps Angus would like her to cut off his head.

I cheered, but of course that was the only sentence Aunt Maggie heard, and she was shocked to find Annette threatening death by axe blade.

"And I want you to meet Charlie's new wife, Annette," she said, in the tone you would use if your brother had married a potential murderer, "and his son, Angus, and his daughter Shelley. My other niece, Joanna, I'm sorry to say, is in France, staying with the children's mother. It's one of these . . ." Aunt Maggie paused.

Broken family situations, I thought.

Annette flushed, and Angus flipped to a new page in his notebook.

I wanted to talk back to Aunt Maggie. Daddy didn't trust you with the truth about Toby, I thought. Or else he forgot about you and just didn't bother.

"And these are Joel and Beth Schmidt," Aunt Maggie finished the introduction. "Beth dated your father in high school."

"Pre-Celeste?" said Angus, interested.

Everybody laughed. "Very pre-Celeste," agreed Beth.

I looked at her with fascination. She wore many rings on each hand, around which the flesh bulged with fat. Her hair was partly gray and held down with bobby pins, and she was still pretending to be a size twelve and wearing the dress she had bought when she was a size twelve, and she looked awful. I bet Daddy wouldn't recognize her. I bet they would have to introduce him to Beth, and he would certainly rejoice in his decision to stop dating her.

Beth leaned back against Joel's equally large stomach. "We were such good friends with your real mother, Shelley. And of course I hope we'll be such good friends with your stepmother, too." She smiled brightly.

For a minute I wanted to kick her in her fat shins. But only for a minute.

No doubt about it: When a man marries three times, it's awkward for the old friends and the family. So I forgave the woman, because at least she was saying she liked my mother. But then Aunt Maggie said to Beth, "They have a hard time dealing with being a broken family. You have to be understanding."

Annette grabbed Angus's wrist, which was a good move, because sharp pencils can be as bad as axes.

Maybe people from stable families can be understanding. Maybe all those backyards naturally make you understanding. I wouldn't know. I'm new to backyards. "We are not broken, Aunt Maggie. Plates get broken. Glasses get broken. Legs get broken. Families do not get broken." Angus pantomimed that we would be happy to break legs or plates. "And if anything is broken around here, it's your family," I said. "And you're too cowardly to admit it."

Aunt Maggie gasped.

Beth and Joel said hastily that perhaps they would just go and refill their drinks.

Last year, when we were renting a place in Vermont, before we bought our own cottage, the lawn mower flicked a pebble against the dining room sliding glass door. For a moment, it was just a hole with a few little cuts radiating off it. But as we watched, the cuts grew. Shatter lines laced across the glass and linked up with each other, and slowly the entire huge door became a sea of glassy cracks. It didn't fall apart. But you couldn't see through it anymore.

That was me. Shattered. When Mommy left Daddy to go with Jean-Paul, the cuts grew and connected until I was all one frosty collection of splinters.

We *were* broken.

At last, I could admit it. But families have strong glue. I'd been repaired. Just this summer. Just this day.

There we stood: Aunt Maggie, Annette, Angus and me.

"You're right, Shelley," whispered my aunt. "I'm sorry for saying that. I know I get overbearing. I guess I'm still hoping we haven't actually broken—Brett and I." Aunt Maggie held out her arms to me.

For a long minute I stared at her empty arms. I could hardly tell whose they were: Aunt Maggie's or my mother's. I stepped inside the circle of her arms and she closed them around me, and our hug was a rocking hug, a dancing hug. A good hug.

"Maggie!" called Uncle Todd. "Ellen is here!"

Aunt Maggie let me go. She walked toward her husband thickly, as if she were swimming.

"Guess what, Annette!" I said, wanting to share the good news with her. I felt bright from the inside out. I knew that my eyes were shining, and my hair was shining, and my heart. "I'm going to visit Mommy after all, Annette, this very summer. What do you think? Isn't that great? My own mother! I'm okay about it now!"

Annette burst into tears.

Chapter Thirteen

People's emotions are always lying there, waiting for you to step on them and muddy them up and squash them beneath your feet.

"Annette, stop crying," I said, shoving her into the house. "People will see you; they'll think there's something wrong. They already don't understand about Daddy because of Toby and because of Angus being weird." I herded Annette to the safety of the back hall, where we wouldn't run into anybody.

"I thought you and I were getting along so well," Annette said, weeping. "Who's Toby?"

"Toby is not Daddy's son," I reassured her. "And we *are*

getting along so well. That's the whole point. So I'm calling her Mommy again."

Annette said if he didn't get here soon, she was going to have a complete and total nervous breakdown.

"If who doesn't get here soon?" I asked. "Toby?"

"Who is Toby?" exclaimed Annette. "Why would I care about this Toby? Your father, of course! And what made you suddenly want to visit France? You won't even get on the phone with your mother."

"I know, but I'm the prodigal daughter. Or she's the prodigal mother. We're going to party. I can tell. I'm ready."

"I thought you were the stable one," said Annette gloomily. "Are you just starting a mental collapse, Shelley, or are you well into it?"

"You thought I was the stable one?"

Angus joined us.

"Go away," I said to him.

"No. Why is Annette crying? Do you want to see my autograph collection?"

"Angus, did you ask anybody how many wives they've had?" I demanded.

"No, what do you think, that I'm weird or something?"

Annette began laughing insanely.

"Don't laugh like that, Annette," said Angus. "People will think you're weird."

"People would be right. I'm going to wash my face."

Annette headed for the stairs and the bathroom least likely to be occupied, but a pack of guests who had been touring the house were coming down. She headed for the family room, but a pack of guests who were sick of the mosquitoes outside had filled it up.

My grandmother emerged from the formal living room. My aunt and uncle have one of these houses where nobody ever uses the living room. You look in the door, as if you're at a historical house with velvet ropes to block passage, but you never go in. "Annette, darling," said Grandma, "come sit with me for a minute. You look a little strung out."

We all went into the living room. Delicately, because Aunt Maggie would be able to see our footprints in the nap of the carpet.

Grandma said she had been crying herself just a little bit. "People always cry at reunions," she said. "Like weddings. Or funerals. There's something very painful and very beautiful about your very own family."

Annette turned her face to the wall.

It's not her very own family, I thought. There's nothing beautiful here for her. All she has is trouble.

Annette turned back to face us again, and somehow she had gotten strength from checking out the wallpaper. Maybe we should take a roll of it home. "I'm just frazzled from the plane flight," she said. We let it pass.

Angus said he wanted to know what stable meant, anyhow. It seemed to be the most important word in Barrington conversations.

"It means you are not affected by change," said Grandma. "In physics it means the atoms don't decay. They just go on and on, always the same."

"How boring," said my brother. "And here I thought it was good to be stable. You mean all stable is, is that every morning you wake up and there's nothing new? But I like change."

Grandma looked as if she wanted to take all three of us, one by one, including Annette, onto her lap for snuggling. Annette just looked as if she wanted the next flight out. "Who is Toby, anyhow?" Annette said. "And what do you mean, he isn't your father's son?"

I told them everything.

Angus, with the same interest he had shown in Vermont, namely very little, said, "That was pretty nice of Dad, huh?"

Annette said, "Yes, he's like that."

And I said, "But why was it a secret when it's so nice? I thought you only kept bad things secret."

"Barrington gave your father a pain in the neck, just the way it did Celeste," said Grandma, laughing. "Just the way it did me. Why do you think I moved to Arizona? Everybody in Barrington always has to be knowing things."

At last Angus was fascinated. "You mean you lied when you said you moved because the winters here are so hard?"

"The winters are hard, but eighty years in Barrington were enough. For your father, sixteen years were enough. He liked to keep his life to himself. You can't do that in a small town."

Grandma forgave him, I thought. He ran away all those years ago and had divorces and troubles and gave her grief, and she doesn't care. "Does Aunt Maggie know about Toby?" I asked.

"We all know about Toby. He's spent every summer of his life here with his grandparents, and half of it on my front porch."

"Drinking lemonade." I nodded, envying Toby.

"But I doubt if Maggie knew your father supported Toby and Celeste for several years. Your father didn't think it was anybody's business. I don't think he would consider it a secret, just something in the past between him and Celeste." Grandma looked soft and sad.

"Are you crying, Grandma?" I said.

"Yes, honey. I'm proud of your father."

"He's pretty great, huh, Annette?" Angus said.

Annette shrugged.

"Just because you have to party without him," said Angus, "is no reason to get mad at him."

"She's upset because I'm going to visit Mom after all," I said. "But how come, Annette? Why aren't you glad?"

She shrugged.

"Love isn't flat, like a freshly ironed sheet, Shelley," said my grandmother. But it was Annette's hand that her gnarled fingers took and held. "Love is a tangle. Hair that's never been brushed."

Annette said, "I thought I was more important. I guess in spite of all my best intentions about keeping my perspective, I decided I came first."

Angus explained to her that stepmothers never came first. She nodded. "I know."

"But you come in second," Angus told her. "Second is pretty high, when you consider the population of the United States."

Out in the yard we heard a tremendous hullabaloo.

People were shouting, yelling, cheering.

"What's that?" said Angus, obviously hoping for a fire or an explosion to liven things up. He leaped away, grateful for an excuse to abandon all these emotional women cluttering up the place, and raced out.

Grandma stood up, taking my arm for support. "Might as well see what all the commotion is about," she said.

Annette followed without enthusiasm, as if any commotion Barrington might rustle up was assuredly not going to be worth the trip.

Aunt Maggie, who must have been showing off bedroom décor, came hurtling down the stairs. She was horrified by the idea that yet another major catastrophe had happened at her party. All of us hit the back door together.

"Surprise!" shouted my father.

He stood at the edge of the yard, tall and heavy and laughing. He shouted out the names of all those old friends and yelled hello to his sister Maggie and bellowed with joy at the sight of the dessert table and the welcome-home icing on the big sheet cake.

Angus threw himself on Daddy. "You lied," said Angus. "You said you weren't coming for days."

"Are you kidding? Ruin your aunt Maggie's surprise party? I just had to add a little extra excitement to the event."

"You were coming all along?" cried Angus joyfully. "You were just giving your own sister a hard time? Like a real brother and sister?" He and Daddy laughed and socked each other.

"Should I beat him black and blue," said Aunt Maggie to Grandma and me and Annette, "or join in the hugging?"

Grandma began laughing. It was that soft, possessive love of people who had always known what Daddy was like, but now they knew again.

"Annette, did you know all along?" I accused her.

She rolled her eyes. "Of course. He thought it was funny."

How maddening for her, listening to Aunt Maggie carry on. She could have given Daddy away. I bet she wanted to. But she stuck on his side, even though he was being as much of a pain as Angus ever was.

Aunt Maggie began to laugh, just when I had thought she would never have a real, true laugh again in this world. She and my father went toward each other carefully, miming a fight. "Charlie," she said to him, "I don't know how yet, but you are going to pay."

The guests egged her on, with a dozen suggestions of what could be done to my father. Angus whipped out his notebook and wrote them all down.

I wanted to race up like Angus and fling myself on top of Daddy and be his special girl in front of everybody. But I didn't. I could feel Annette wanting to do the same thing. But she didn't. It was like opening the door for somebody, where you each step back and wait for the other person to go first.

Daddy is first for both of us, I thought. And we don't know how to share very well. And Joanna can't share at all.

But the first one of us Daddy kissed was his mother, my grandmother. He swung her on his arm and then put the other arm around Annette. Grandma slipped free, and I had a turn with the arm she had used. Even Daddy's one-armed hugs are bear hugs. "Daddy," I said reproachfully, "you made us suffer. We had to listen to Aunt Maggie say bad things about you."

Daddy roared with laughter.

I didn't have to protect him, I thought. Daddy never cared what anybody here thought. Only I cared.

Carolyn came over for her hug, but she was shy about it. My father is so much more energetic than her father. Daddy shook hands with Uncle Todd, and then finally he said, "Maggie, don't be mad. I had to do it to you. The situation begged for it."

Behind her, their friends began singing "For She's a Jolly Good Fellow." Maggie allowed my father to kiss her cheek. She called him some names, and people with video cameras told her to talk louder so they could immortalize it.

"Your son," said Aunt Maggie, as if Angus were a clear and present danger, "has a present for you. Autographs of everybody in town." She moved into the shadows, letting my father have the stage he was so good at taking, and Uncle Todd put his arm around his wife's waist.

Angus displayed his autograph collection proudly. He looked with satisfaction at the gathering of relatives. "We're all here now," he said contentedly. Then he left us, because a latecomer had brought yet another dessert.

Angus's sentence hit me. We're all here now.

But we weren't all here. Joanna, our sister, she wasn't here. Mommy, our real mother, she wasn't here.

All my family reunions will be partial, I thought.

What will my wedding be like one day? Extra pews for extra families? Double-length inscriptions on the invitations to accommodate all the parents?

Oh, Brett. Oh, Joanna. Don't fall out the bottom of our families. Come home.

I thought of Aunt Maggie having to look at the videos and photographs of this party, which was going to be a smashing success and remembered by all. But forever and ever the photographs would remind her that one summer she was missing a son.

The party changed.

Laughter was longer and louder, the way laughter is when my father is there, and the stories were funnier, and the food even yummier. The heat did not lessen, but nobody went into the air-conditioning now; everybody gathered around Daddy and told stories and shouted out punch lines and passed drinks and barbecue and extra napkins.

"Shelley, there's a call for you," said Carolyn. "It's a boy."

"Toby?"

"No. Weird name. I had to ask three times to be sure of it. DeWitt?"

"DeWitt!" I said. "What phone did he call on?"

"Your cell phone, of course. It's in my room. A guest heard it ringing and tracked it down and reported in." The two of us ran to her bedroom, where none other than Beth, the pre-Celeste girlfriend, was chatting away with DeWitt. "Well, I am just so glad I found out where you got that name from, DeWitt," said Beth. "Now here's Shelley, at last. I declare, they had to go all the way to Texas to find her."

"DeWitt?" I said into the phone.

Beth grinned at me and said, "Carolyn, let's go have a

dessert," and all of a sudden I thought, Daddy's pre-Celeste girlfriend was pretty good too.

"It's me," confirmed DeWitt. "How are you doing?"

"Is it an emergency?" I asked him. "Did our house burn down? Or yours? Are you all right?"

"I just wanted to say hi. See how it's going. And if Annette sagged and Toby turned out to be your brother."

"Oh, DeWitt, you won't believe it. Toby's not my brother, but he is the son of Daddy's first wife, except his father of course was the second husband. I know, there are a lot of husbands and wives in my story, you don't have to remind me, they play my family here like a board game. Toby is really nice. I went on a roller coaster with him." I could see DeWitt, his shaggy hair, his face with too much forehead until his smile equaled it out, like an equation in math. "DeWitt, I don't think I gave you my cell phone number."

"You didn't. I asked the Frankels. They have about sixty-two numbers for you guys. Five cell phones, New York home phone, Vermont home phone, Paris home phone, Barrington home phone. In case of emergency, they'd probably be on the phone two or three days just trying to break through."

I was grinning all over my entire body. Especially my nice bare midriff. I wished DeWitt could see me in my wonderful yellow dress. "How was the hike?"

"It was good. I held up best. I was strongest. We didn't

meet anything scary, though. No bears. And guess what. The Lake Association hired me to paint docks for the rest of the summer, so I'll be here when you get back after all."

"That's wonderful! And my cousin Carolyn is coming back with us. And then I think for a week I'll go to France to visit my mother. I can't wait to see you. My whole life has changed in this visit. I'll tell you everything when I get back."

"Great," said DeWitt hesitantly, as if he had something else to say.

I waited, but he didn't say it. "Bye," I said, and the syllable was lame and pitiful, and it needed other things on both sides of it.

"Bye," said DeWitt, and there was another pause full of things we meant to say, and then we both hung up. I stared at the phone in my hand as if it were as special as the necklace Grandma had given me.

Carolyn flung herself back into the room. Only Beth had gone downstairs.

"Was that your boyfriend?" Carolyn burst out. "You didn't tell me you have a boyfriend. I can't believe you've been here all this time and you didn't tell me about your boyfriend."

All this time.

I had been in Barrington two days.

"Why didn't you tell me?" demanded Carolyn.

I didn't want to say that I had not mentioned my boyfriend because I had not known that he was one. "I guess we hadn't gotten to that yet," I said. "You know. We would have. Later."

Carolyn sighed happily. "It was too intimate to talk about until you knew me better and trusted me completely. Will you tell me absolutely everything later on?" She leaned forward and stared into my eyes in a meaningful way. "I want to know how, Shelley."

I kind of wanted to know how myself. I didn't think a description of DeWitt's hands on my knees was what Carolyn had in mind.

We floated back into the party. DeWitt had gone to the trouble of getting my phone number from the Frankels, all because he wanted to make sure I knew he was going to be at the lake after all. I would have two more reunions, one with DeWitt and one with my mother.

Carolyn was floating along for other reasons. She thought I was going to tell her all about sex. I had a good book to recommend to her, but it was back in New York.

The party was over.

The guests had gone home.

It was three in the morning.

Angus had fallen asleep on the grass, and Daddy maneuvered him to bed. Grandma had hardly stayed up at all after Daddy arrived. I couldn't imagine being tired just when the party really took off, but Grandma said when you were eighty, you could even be too tired for parties. Carolyn and I dragged huge black plastic garbage bags around the yard, stuffing them full of used paper napkins, paper cups, paper plates and plastic spoons. Annette covered miles of uneaten spareribs in plastic wrap while Daddy was having an argument with Aunt Maggie.

"Why are you mad at me?" he said. "I thought it was funny. I swore Annette to secrecy, and I didn't even let Angus and Shelley in on the joke."

Aunt Maggie was crying. This had been a very tear-filled reunion so far, and we were only at the top of day two.

"It was the best party ever," protested my father.

Aunt Maggie continued to cry.

"Okay, I'm sorry," said my father. "It was juvenile. It was dumb. I admit it. But that's the kind of family we always were, Maggie. I was always getting into trouble, and you were always having to handle it, and I figured it would be like old times, and you'd laugh about it, and—"

"You are such a conceited person, Charlie Wollcott. If you think I have time to worry about your inconsiderate stupid pranks, you are wrong. I am worried about my son. The Camerons told him to leave and he did. But he didn't come home. He's not here. He could be anywhere. Hitchhiking, getting picked up by mass murderers or rapists of young boys. And you're playing silly games."

Uncle Todd sighed. "Maggie, you're getting melodramatic.

I'm sure Brett just moved on to another friend's house. He's popular, you know. After he wears out his welcome at one place, he can just move on to another."

"That's even worse," cried Aunt Maggie. "There won't be a street in town where I can drive without wondering if my own son is living there."

"In the morning we'll find him," said Uncle Todd.

"You're not even worried!" she accused him.

"I'm worried about us," said Uncle Todd. "I'm worried about putting this family back together. But I'm not worried about Brett. He's not going to do anything foolish like vanish across the horizon, Maggie. He has another ball game to coach and he has to be at work. I'll just go down to the warehouse in the morning and have a talk with him."

Aunt Maggie stared at a vast tray of leftover foods Annette was preparing to squeeze into the refrigerator. "This was supposed to be such a wonderful week. All spring I planned a celebration of our anniversary and Charlie's welcome home and a family reunion. But it's my family that isn't together."

I turned quickly to help Annette shift things in the refrigerator.

I couldn't look at my aunt.

I had wanted something like this to happen to them, so they wouldn't be Perfect anymore.

Chapter Fourteen

I began my e-mail to Joanna shortly after breakfast. It was the longest e-mail in the history of the Wollcott family. It was more like an encyclopedia entry.

. . . so Daddy comforted Annette that she is still very important and probably the major cause in my coming to terms with Mommy and Jean-Paul, and Annette being so stable is probably the most vital part of our family right now. Annette liked that, and luckily Angus didn't argue. I could have, but I didn't, which I feel was mature of me. You have to give Annette another chance, Jo. She really is very decent. And then I told Daddy and Annette how DeWitt had telephoned and wants me to go out with him once I'm back in Vermont. And Annette told Daddy about the engagement necklace Grandma gave me and how we're going to shop for a really special dress for the dance, and Daddy said, "What dance?" and Annette explained, "There isn't one yet," and Daddy said, "Perhaps we should give the dance!" and Annette said, "No, the lake is not the kind of location for the kind of dance for the kind of dress that would suit the engagement necklace." Daddy said he gave up. Angus said if DeWitt and I get married, I have to promise not to name our son DeWitt because there is such a thing as going too far.

I stopped writing.

What would Grandma give Joanna that could possibly be the equal of my necklace? Joanna is the oldest grandchild. Grandma couldn't have left Joanna out, could she? Was there a family rule that if you skipped the reunion, you didn't get a good present? Would Grandma send Joanna a pair of socks from the discount mall?

"Who are you writing to, sugar?" asked my father, coming up behind me and kissing my hair eleven times.

"Joanna. I'm telling her about the necklace and the party and DeWitt and how I'm going to France now too, which reminds me, Daddy. Telephone Mother right now and let her know the dates I'm visiting."

"Your mother would be a lot more thrilled if you made the call."

"If I call now, I've wasted my entire e-mail."

Daddy laughed. "Finish the e-mail. Send it. Then we'll both call. I knew when you finally took off, it would be like a volcano, Shell, but I didn't think it would happen in only two days while I wasn't here to see it."

"I haven't told you about the real explosion."

He hit his head in mock horror. "Are you going to take over Angus's slot in life now? You're going to be the one to start things?"

I nodded.

"Well, whatever it is, you look pretty happy about it. Tell me."

"I have a date for a drive this afternoon."

"A date! Who on earth have you met and gotten that close to in forty-eight hours?"

"Toby. He's wonderful. We got talking because I hadn't understood the gossip about him. In fact, Daddy, you omitted to tell me that he even existed to start with, which, I have to tell you, hurt his feelings very much. I comforted him. Angus and I had thought maybe Toby was actually your son, and therefore our brother, and—"

"Toby?" said my father, thunderstruck. *"You have a date with Toby? Celeste's son? That Toby?"*

"Of course that Toby."

"No!" shouted my father. "No, you can't do that. You certainly can't go around in a car with him offering him comfort."

"Daddy! He wants to meet you. You'll like him a lot."

"I'm not ready for this."

"Sixteen years and you're not ready?"

"You can't go for a drive with him. Now or ever. Shelley, I know better than anybody what happens when—" He was too appalled to finish his sentence. "Well . . . when Celeste and I went for drives—and this is her son—and you're my daughter—no. Never. Forget it. I'm putting you on a plane for Paris right now."

"Daddy, I hardly know Toby, and really and truly, all we're going to do is go for a drive."

"One thing leads to another."

"Not that fast. Don't look so sick. He is a great person."

My father really did look sick. "I don't want you making every mistake that I made. This is too close to home. My daughter dating the son of my first wife? Shelley—no." He looked at Annette for backup. She gestured with hands, face, eyes and elbows that this was his problem, not hers.

"All my life," said my father, "I've coped with Joanna and with Angus, and before them I coped with your mother, and before her I coped with Celeste. But Shelley, you're my easy one. You're my stable one."

"I hate that word *stable*."

"I know a person gets tired of the concept, but still—"

"I hate being counted on! I want to be the one who does stuff you don't expect. Grandma explained the chemistry to us. A stabilizer keeps a mixture from being changed by new additions. I'm sick of being the stabilizer."

My father said gloomily, "I don't see anything good coming of this."

"Daddy, you were the one who was so nice to Toby. You paid to take care of him when he was little and Celeste was going to law school, and you were totally wonderful, and I'm proud of that, and Toby turned out to be a wonderful person too. And he asked me to go out with him. So there."

Actually he had not asked me to go out with him. He had asked to continue our conversation, except in a car with him driving. I thought that Toby probably just wanted to discuss family history in detail, and I *really* thought Toby was just hoping my father would be standing in the driveway, and they could meet at last.

. . . and then, Joanna, Daddy began telling me about Sunday school. They're really into Sunday school around here. Daddy says you're not supposed to let your right hand know what your left hand is doing. I said, "What on earth does that mean? If you're driving and your right hand doesn't know that your left hand is turning the steering wheel, there's going to be an accident." Daddy said real charity does not brag, even to itself. He said when you're doing a kindness, boasting ruins it. So with one hand, you write the check, and with the other hand, you block your own sight of it. Isn't that neat?

So I said, "How come you never took us to Sunday school when you learned so much important stuff there?" He said when he left Barrington, he really left Barrington, and that included things like Sunday school that symbolized Barrington.

"You don't like Barrington?" I said to him. I wished he could see Barrington the way I used to, with front porches and lemonade and hugs, a time of summer and happiness.

"I'm starting to like Barrington again," he said. "I went through a long, heavy-duty rebellion. It lasted for years. I didn't actually want this reunion. Not that I wasn't glad to get together with my family again, but I didn't much want to remember the details of my teenage years again."

"But everybody was so glad to see you, Daddy! You were the star of the show!"

"It's tough growing up, Shell. Or haven't you noticed?"

"I noticed."

"It takes most people a couple of years. Took me a couple of decades. Nobody really wants to go back and stand where he was jeered at and mocked when he was a kid."

I could not believe this. "What did they jeer at you for?"

"Getting married at sixteen. Dropping out of school. Being a failure. Bringing embarrassment and rage to our families. Going on welfare."

"Daddy! You were on welfare?"

"Just for a little while. Celeste and I had absolutely no idea how to be grown-ups. So we quit trying. She went to live with her aunt in Chicago, and I went to New York and lived with a bunch of young guys as worthless as I was and didn't make the slightest attempt to be adult again until I met your mother."

. . . we talked for hours, Jo. I love hearing stories about when Daddy was little. Of course, he wasn't little during these stories—he was a teenager—but he sounds so little. And so dumb. Every story

179

he told, I wanted to go, "But Daddy, how could you have done so many things wrong in such a short time?" Anyway, he was pretty set against my going anywhere with Toby. But he didn't want to refuse me either, so he's letting me go. But he's not going to meet Toby. He says life is emotional enough without that.

So here's my schedule for the next fifteen minutes:
1. send this to you
2. telephone Mother and tell her I'm visiting her, and that Carolyn is coming too, although we haven't asked Aunt Maggie yet, but I figure if we already have Mother's permission, we're set, so you get started on that
3. drive with Toby

Chapter Fifteen

Toby was a good driver. We drove all over the countryside, he gripping the wheel and me over by my window. He talked on and on about mothers and fathers. I was ready to talk about boys and girls, but Toby gave no sign that he was tired of the parental subject. "My grandparents wanted me to bring you over so they could meet you," he confided, "but I said maybe later."

"Why do they want to meet me?" I said cautiously.

"Because if your father had stayed married to my mother, you'd be their granddaughter."

"Genes don't work that way," I pointed out. "Still, it's nice to know they liked Daddy. I thought nobody wanted Celeste and my father to get married."

"Nobody wanted them to get married at sixteen. But other than that, it was fine."

We broke up laughing. "Keep steering," I said. "Or we'll get killed. Too much laughing on the part of the driver is against the rules."

"You know, only people like us really know how to laugh," said Toby. "I know this girl who is another Perfect, just like your aunt Maggie, and she takes everything so seriously."

"Poor Aunt Maggie. She's so broken up about Brett."

"I don't blame her. Brett is being a jerk. But you know, sometimes I think in families where nothing has ever gone wrong, when even the littlest thing does go wrong, the families collapse. Brett could always be pretty good at stuff without half trying. He was never the best, because for that you actually have to try. But he could always hang out with the best, whether it was in golf or math. So he gets behind the wheel of a car, and he's a terrible driver, and whoever wanted to admit to being a terrible driver? Brett never seems able to tell where the edge of his car is, which is key if you want to miss other people's cars. So Brett keeps having accidents and almost hits people and his father takes away the car and Brett's so mad he won't stay home. Of course, he doesn't get mad at his father, he gets mad at his mother, who had nothing to do with the whole car issue. So he's just being a spoiled brat. Don't worry about him."

"Okay," I agreed. I figured I had so many worthwhile people to worry about, why give Brett worrying space? Let Miranda worry about Brett.

"Listen," said Toby.

I listened.

He didn't say anything else.

We both laughed. Giggled, almost. I hadn't been around an older boy who laughed like that. He was really nervous, or that particular sound wouldn't come out. "I'm listening," I said.

"I'm not ready to talk yet."

"Okay, then I won't listen."

Toby cleared his throat. "My mother is a basket case. I phoned her to say that you and I were going for a drive, and she said, 'Charlie's daughter?' "

"That's exactly what my father said! 'Celeste's son? Never! No! One thing leads to another!' "

Toby said, "My mother is convinced you and I are going to run away and get married."

"No, because I won't be sixteen for a year and three quarters, and the running-away tradition is age sixteen."

"Rats. We'll have to postpone it, then."

. . . I know, Joanna, this is another encyclopedia-sized e-mail. But there's so much to say, and I like looking at my words on the screen and seeing what I'm thinking.

And then Toby said his mother decided she needed him back in Chicago to help out. "Help out how?" I asked Toby, and he said, "Help her not worry that I'm going to make the same mistakes she did." I said, "Every grown-up in Barrington is obsessive about that. All Aunt Maggie can say is that Brett is making the same mistakes my father did."

"Oh, right," Toby said, "like she didn't have any mistakes in her past that Brett could possibly repeat."

And then a funny thing happened, Jo. We were both ready to say good-bye. Good-bye for good. I think maybe we really were related, in a way; at least, we shared a lot. We shared Daddy, a past, secrets—good secrets. Toby was like a cousin or a brother. I'm crazy about Toby and yet I wanted to say good-bye. Plus, of course, I have DeWitt waiting for me out on the lake. I guess it's easier to do anything when somebody is waiting for you

I skipped telling Joanna about one part of the good-bye.

Toby kissed me. It was a real kiss. A boy-loves-girl kiss. I had never had one before. In one soft touch of my lips to his, I knew why Daddy ran away with Celeste, and I knew why Daddy and Celeste were both afraid to have Toby and me in the same car.

I wanted to kiss like that all my life . . . and yet . . . maybe not with Toby.

"Next summer?" he said. "Will you be visiting the Perfects again next summer?"

I nodded. I didn't want to speak. I wanted my lips to remember the kiss. He was very flushed. He turned the air-conditioning in the car up higher and cranked the volume on the radio and drove me back home.

Home.

Aunt Maggie and Uncle Todd's, really.

And yet there is something about relatives that makes their house your house. It was home. It didn't have the wide front porch or the lemonade, but it had family.

"This is only my third day in Barrington," I said. "It feels like my third year."

Toby laughed. "I've always felt that way about this town. It's so slow. Nothing ever happens."

It seemed to me that more had happened in Barrington than usually happened in a year. I felt I had shot right through my father's adolescence and grown up through three or four years of my own.

We pulled up in front of Aunt Maggie's, but Toby didn't turn into the driveway.

"Bye," I said softly.

He sat on his side of the front seat, looking neither left nor right. He had no intention of making eye contact with me. I was hurt. Then I saw, gathering a few feet away in the driveway, my whole family. Grandma, Aunt Maggie, Carolyn, Annette and Daddy were getting ready to go somewhere in his rental car.

"You want to meet Daddy?" I said to Toby.

"Not with that audience."

"I don't blame you. I'll hop out. You can drive away and pretend you didn't see them."

Toby swallowed. "Okay."

I opened my door.

But it didn't work that easily. What ever does? My father left the group, walked over to us and came around to the driver's side. "Hello, Toby," he said, bending over and putting out his right hand. "I've always wanted to meet you. It's a privilege."

I finished getting out.

My father said, "I gather it's been a pretty emotional weekend here, Toby. I don't want you to be left with worries or questions. How about you and I go have a hamburger somewhere and talk? Or would that upset your mother?"

Toby shrugged the way Angus used to when he was very little, not because he didn't care, but because words were too much for him.

Daddy got into the passenger seat where I had been and

told me he'd be back in an hour or so and why didn't I go shopping with the girls?

. . . so the unfair part, Joanna, totally unfair, is that none of us know what Daddy and Toby talked about. I mean of course I do know; I know they talked about Celeste and Daddy's marriage, and divorce, and why he helped her out with expenses all those years ago. But I didn't get to be there and hear his exact words and see if Daddy, who hugs us all the time, hugged Toby. As if Toby could have been his son and, maybe in a tiny distant way, is his son.

We went shopping instead. Antiquing, actually. A long row of shops in a little village near Barrington, filled with dusty old stuff Annette kept saying would look perfect at the summer house and Aunt Maggie kept saying were too high priced and Grandma kept saying she used to have when she was a little girl. I was megabored. My head was crammed full of thoughts about Daddy and Toby and you and Mother and Jean-Paul and Brett, all of you tumbling and whirling like clothes in a dryer . . .

* * *

In one of the antique shops, I said, "Are you going back to work, Annette? Did you decide?"

Annette nodded. "Yes. I am. I loved my job, you know. And I was good at it. It's nice to do things you're good at."

I fingered the back of the old kitchen chair Annette said she would buy if we had come by car and she had any way to get it to Vermont. It looked to me like an ordinary chair, not worth toting a couple thousand feet, let alone miles.

We were eye level. Annette is exactly my height. We could share clothes, I thought suddenly. The world seemed full of things I had not yet shared with Annette. "I kind of wish you weren't going back to work," I said. "It was fun with you home. In Vermont."

We drove back to the Preffyns', and there on the sidewalk was Angus walking in the other direction. He didn't see us, and he didn't change his manner even when we slowed down. He wore a hot pink T-shirt he had cut into shreds, so that pink ribbons blew around his chest. He had on baggy orange-and-red shorts. Carolyn had braided string bracelets in purple and black around his wrists, and Angus had not let her cut off the ends, so his wrists dripped cords. He had slashed open the toes on a pair of high-top sneakers Brett had discarded and left in the garage, and the sneakers flapped like mouths with sock tongues, and he was dancing to make them flap even more. He had his leg slung over his shoulder. I had forgotten about the leg. Every time he hopped, the leg kicked him in the behind.

"How do you live with that?" Aunt Maggie said seriously to Annette.

Annette said she was getting used to it.

I said I personally would never get used to it.

Aunt Maggie began a long story about how my father used to humiliate her when they were about ten and twelve years old. Grandma kept adding details and correcting Aunt Maggie: "No, dear, it was on Elm Street, not Lincoln, remember? In front of the Stevensons' house."

Angus spotted us. Immediately his plans changed. He switched direction and began running alongside the car, his leg bouncing against his back, and his sneakers flapping. "Time my speed!" he screamed.

"The leg is slowing you down!" yelled Carolyn. "Pass it through the window."

He passed it through the window, and Carolyn held it. It was good that Annette was driving, because Aunt Maggie would have insisted on a full stop and a careful exchange.

"How fast am I going?" shrieked Angus, his load lightened.

"Ninety miles an hour!" screamed Annette.

"Tell the truth!" shrieked Angus.

"No," said Annette. "Nobody else bothers with that around here. Why should I?"

We crept down the street while Angus ran, and car and boy arrived home together. Carolyn and I changed into our swimsuits and swam in the backyard pool because we didn't want to run into Brett or Miranda. Annette said definitely Carolyn must spend the rest of August with us. We'd be in Vermont for ten days, and then Annette would drive us down to New York and over to Kennedy Airport and put Carolyn and me on the plane for Paris.

"What?" said Aunt Maggie, who had been left out of this particular loop.

"I haven't actually called my mother yet," I said nervously.

"I called," said Annette. "She's thrilled. She can't wait to have three girls to play with in Paris. I talked to Joanna, too. She's a little bored on her own. She needs you and Carolyn."

"Annette," I said, "you are awesome. Making that call for me."

"I'm not making the next call, Shelley. I think your mother is sitting by the phone. Hoping."

A little shiver ran through me.

My mother, sitting across an ocean. Waiting. Hoping. For me.

I didn't feel I should be the only one to suffer, though. Let her wait and hope. It was her turn.

Angus lit the grill so Uncle Todd could broil the chicken that had been marinating. Aunt Maggie put on a huge pot of water to boil for corn on the cob that Grandma had bought at the farmers' market. Daddy woke up from a nap and asked for lemonade.

I said, "Can we squeeze the lemons?"

Grandma said she thought she could remember how to cut a lemon in half. So we made lemonade.

Daddy and I took our lemonades into the shade. "Now the reunion is perfect," I said. "Real lemonade. If only Brett would come home."

Daddy said not all family reunions happened when you wanted them to. That Brett might be home in an hour or a year. I said, "Can't we help?" and Daddy said no, because he had spent a good deal of his life telling his Barrington relations to butt out of his child-rearing decisions, and he could hardly butt into this one. Anyway, said Daddy, Uncle Todd and Brett were doing just fine together. Uncle Todd was taking Brett out for breakfast every morning. Which naturally just made Aunt Maggie feel ten times worse. It was her demand for Perfection that was driving Brett crazy. Things weren't as bad as they seemed.

"I don't want you to worry, so I'm letting you in on it, Shelley," said my father. "The fact is that sometimes fathers and sons have to settle things alone, without the women." He looked at me rather sadly. "And sometimes, mothers and daughters do too. I'm glad you're going to France."

"What if it doesn't work? What if I'm still mad at Mommy?"

"It's only for a week. Go see the Eiffel Tower instead of your mother. But I think it will work. I think you're both ready."

"Are you still mad at Mommy?"

My father was silent for a long time. "Honey, I can go back into the past and be mad at the sixteen-year-old boy who wouldn't do the dishes and threw the plates against the wall instead and made a sixteen-year-old girl so mad she went to live with her aunt. I can go back into the past and be mad at your mother for finding somebody more elegant and worldly than I am. But I love the family I have now. I love the people that you and Joanna and Angus have grown up to be. I love Annette. So mostly, no. I'm not mad. And I don't want you to be mad either, honey. Being mad takes up so much energy. It's hard to be yourself when you're furious all the time. You weren't yourself, you know. You lived through Angus and you lived through Joanna, but you didn't really live as Shelley. This weekend"—my father hugged me as hard as he ever had, so tight I could hardly breathe—"Shelley, my real reunion this weekend is with you."

Chapter Sixteen

The plane was late, of course.

Whenever you're eager to move on to the next phase of your life, the plane is always delayed.

We were waiting in the terminal as if waiting for the dentist. Endless silent staring at the bucket seats opposite, at other people's knees and the backs of their newspapers.

Angus had left his leg in Aunt Maggie's car.

"Don't you want your leg?" she said.

"No, thank you," said Angus. "I think you can throw it in the trash for me. If you would."

All this courtesy made Aunt Maggie suspicious. She thought maybe she should have the security people run the leg through X rays just in case it was something *she* didn't want around either.

"No, really," said Angus. "I've outgrown it. You realize I'm going to be thirteen soon. Thanks for a wonderful visit, Aunt Maggie. You made us all feel so welcome."

"It's me," said Annette. "I've succeeded where thousands failed. I've taught him manners, propriety and common sense."

On our way through security, Angus said to Carolyn, "Don't let anybody see you're reading a guidebook to New York."

"Why not?"

"You don't want anybody thinking you don't know your way around. You want to be cool and experienced."

"Oh," said Carolyn. She flattened the book on itself so that the back cover pressed against the front cover and nobody could guess what she was reading. "Other instructions?" she asked Angus.

"I think we're fine now," said Angus, surveying us carefully.

After we got through security, Daddy bought two newspapers and we trudged to our gate to hear the unwelcome news that we were indefinitely postponed. We sat. We stared. Angus was calm and sober.

Annette began humming softly to herself.

"Annette!" whispered Angus. "Shh. People can hear you."

"Angus, I have quite a nice hum. I'm on pitch and everything."

The waiting area was packed. People had filled all the seats and were leaning on walls and sitting on the carpet and on their luggage, looking morose and sullen.

"People will think you're weird," he said in a low voice.

There was a long silence.

"Angus," I said, "are you embarrassed in public? Is Annette humiliating you with her behavior?"

"Yes."

"Angus, this is a happy day in the family calendar. Revenge is at hand."

Angus looked wary.

"You've been the weird one for twelve years," I told him. "It's my turn." I set my book down. I stood up. I stretched my arms and beat on my chest. "I will start by singing opera. I will stand on my chair and entertain these sorry masses until we board. Some of them will be less grateful than others. I will get autographs from those persons who applaud, however." I cleared my throat. I hummed a pitch to start my aria on.

Angus believed I would do it, because only days ago he would have and loved every minute of it. Today he regarded me with horror. Desperately he looked around for a way to distance himself from this appalling family he seemed to be a member of. "I have to go to the bathroom," he whispered, and he fled before I made a spectacle of myself.

My stepmother, my cousin, my father and I shared the best thing there is to share.

Love and laughter.

About the Author

Caroline B. Cooney is the author of many books for young people, including *Goddess of Yesterday; The Ransom of Mercy Carter; Tune In Anytime; Burning Up; The Face on the Milk Carton* (an IRA-CBC Children's Choice Book) and its companions, *Whatever Happened to Janie?, The Voice on the Radio* (each of them an ALA Best Book for Young Adults) and *What Janie Found; What Child Is This?* (an ALA Best Book for Young Adults); *Driver's Ed* (an ALA Best Book for Young Adults and a *Booklist* Editors' Choice); *Among Friends; Twenty Pageants Later;* and the Time Travel Quartet: *Both Sides of Time, Out of Time, Prisoner of Time* and *For All Time.*

Caroline B. Cooney lives in Westbrook, Connecticut.

Annie Lockwood exists; everyone admits it. Everyone has seen her. But only Strat insists that Miss Lockwood traveled 100 years back in time to be with them in 1895. Now Strat is paying an enormous price; his father has declared him insane and had him locked away in an asylum.

When Time calls Annie back to save Strat, she does not hesitate, even though her family is falling apart and desperately needs her.

Can Annie save the boy she loves, or are she and Strat and her family back home out of time?

Tod Lockwood has never wanted to be anyone's knight in shining armor. In fact, he wants to avoid having anything to do with girls, at least for the present. But that's before Devonny Stratton steps into his life out of the nineteenth century.

As for sixteen-year-old Devonny, she has no plans for marriage until her father arranges to wed her to the contemptuous but well-connected Lord Winden. Devonny has only one hope: Someone must rescue her. Can Tod Lockwood be Time's answer to her prayers? Life never seems simple to Devonny, but do the solutions to her problems await her in the future? Or will she only become a prisoner of a different time?

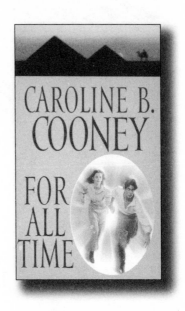

Annie Lockwood is testing Time. She asks to travel back a hundred years to 1899, when her beloved Strat is in Cairo. But in what feels like a cruel joke, Annie is transported to ancient Egypt instead, thousands of years before Strat was born.

Meanwhile, in 1899, Strat is photographing the same pyramids that Annie walks among. And while he eagerly awaits Annie's arrival, another visitor appears: his father, the man who once committed Strat to a mental institution.

Powerless, Annie and Strat both look to Time. Can its force, which brought them together once, help them find each other again?